Only after Dr. Neumann had promised a battery of tests yet to come, and slung the curtain shut behind himself with a metallic screech, could Oliver Brinkman call up the transcript to see the verdict echoed once again upon his contact lenses. Only then did the doctor's words sink in.

"According to the results of your sleep study, Mr. Brinkman, you're brain dead."

ECHOES OF HUSH AND SOLACE

Five extraordinary tales of love, loss, and the paradox of the human condition.

COLLECTED TALES #001

KEN HINCKLEY

Rapid-Dynamix
Publishing

ECHOES OF HUSH AND SOLACE

Published by Rapid-Dynamix Publishing Inc.
www.rapid-dynamix.com
Cover art copyright © 2013 by
Rolffimages | Dreamstime.com
Book and cover design
copyright © 2013 Rapid-Dynamix Publishing

This is the first publication of this collection.

ISBN-13: 978-0615913186
ISBN-10: 0615913180

CONTENTS

Echoes of
Hush and Solace

*Five extraordinary tales of love, loss,
and the paradox of the human condition.*

COLLECTED TALES #001

KEN HINCKLEY

1

BETWEEN GRIEF AND REMEMBRANCE

THE RAINBOW SQUID OF WIRES ERUPTED from the scalp of Oliver Brinkman and into the dark heart of the machine at Dr. Leopold Neumann's feet. The chief attending stood at Oliver's bedside, arms crossed, his name and the logo of the Pacific Northwest Sleep Institute monogrammed on his stark white lab coat.

Oliver couldn't catch the man's eyes. Dr. Neumann seemed intent on finding some unsuspected flaw in the white linoleum, some malignancy in the drab sliding curtains screening the bed from the bustle and aseptic scents of the hallway beyond.

It didn't look like a good sign. Not one bit.

Uh oh, Oliver thought. *My goose is cooked.*

The doctor's hair was wiry and white, combed gruffly across his pale scalp, and his skin was pitted with the acne scars of an ancient youth. The corners of his mouth drained in miniature ravines into the grimace of his face. Dr. Neumann held a puke-green hanging folder in spindly fingers and studied its contents intently, as if there might yet be some reprieve within.

When at last Dr. Neumann spoke, it only took a few brutal seconds of clipped speech to deliver the news. The words made Oliver flinch backwards, like a drink thrown in his face, but they did not yet register. Dr. Neumann scratched his perfectly formed almond-shaped fingernails along the acne pits of his cheek, muttered something about the limits of medicine and science. How he'd never seen anything quite like it. How augmented cognetics and electro-mnemonics had come so far, yet sleep remained the great unknown, the heart of the dark continent.

Only after Dr. Neumann had promised a battery of tests yet to come, and slung the curtain shut behind himself with a metallic screech, could Oliver Brinkman call up the transcript to see the verdict echoed once again upon his contact lenses. Only then did the doctor's words sink in.

"According to the results of your sleep study, Mr. Brinkman, you're brain dead."

* * *

OLIVER DROVE HOME yet did not drive home. Routes recalculated, Oliver's contacts glimmered with arrows pointing the way, but as the first raindrops plummeted through the night and spattered on his sedan's windshield he still knew not where to turn. He drove winding black serpents of suburban blacktop aimlessly, ignoring the street names and trite neighborhood demographics scrolling past. The rain intensified as he tried to lose himself in the maze of meticulously landscaped pedestrian islands and dark cul-de-sacs, even though at some level he knew his electro-mnemonics made it impossible to truly forget where he was. The downpour sheeted across his windshield, transforming the upscale suburban neighborhood into a submerged world of leering windows and ravenous two-story arched foyers that seemed to hunger for his lost soul.

Even his cognitive coprocessors couldn't tell him what he sought; he just didn't know. Roads forked left and right, multiplying endlessly. So many houses. He drove on and on, but there was nowhere to go. No home greeted him, not even his own. Especially not his own.

His apartment stood, he knew, like a cold silent museum of his wife's truncated life, but he couldn't bear to disturb a thing, not one thing. His mnemonics ensured that would remember every last detail, of course, for the rest of his life, but it was the corporeal quality of the objects themselves that had taken on a profound sanctity in his mind of late.

Melissa's book, an antique hardbound volume titled simply *Love Stories*, face-down on her bedside table, the page that marked the day of her death in a high-speed autocrash forever averted from his eyes. Her hairbrush, exactly where she had left it on the bathroom vanity, loose strands of her auburn hair still wound through the bristles. The upright vacuum cleaner, a monument to her fastidiousness. Her bicycle helmet, worn only a handful of times since they'd bought new bikes together the previous spring. A box of white emergency candles, awaiting some contingency that had never arisen. And scores of other things laden with mysterious significance now that she was gone forever.

It was as if the objects, no matter how ordinary, were now sacred vessels imbued with the last vestiges of Melissa's life-force.

So he remembered and he tried to forget and he drove.

He couldn't go back and he couldn't move on. He was a man trapped in the rift between life and death, in the eternal gray penumbral zone between grief and remembrance.

Hours later he watched himself steer back into his apartment complex, as if he were a man detached from his own mind, though he had never made any conscious decision to return home. But there was nowhere else to go. He was new to the Seattle area, he'd lost his well-paying job as a mechanical engineer months ago. And so it was time for the diurnal cycle of his grief to begin anew. It never progressed. Always ended where it started. A bleak undifferentiated eternity without purpose or direction.

He squatted on his couch, elbows on knees, and worked his forehead with cold fingertips as if the grief were a vile black liquid he could express from some vestigial gland concealed beneath the flesh. Without the slightest shift in posture he angled his eyes upward at the two meter wide rectangular abyss of his matte-black television screen. Only a shadowy reflection leered back at him, pupils rolled up nearly into its brows, whites of the eyes glaring back at him like some blank-souled monstrosity of anguish and despair.

On the mantle above the television screen rested the elaborately carved box of Brazilian rosewood. The lid, he knew, was not sealed shut. He could cross the tiny desert of plush taupe carpeting in three strides and open the box at any moment, yet he never did. He had not peered inside in months.

The transparent plastic bag within brimmed with her ashes, but he could not bear to behold them again. The first glance, when he claimed them from the funeral home, had flash-flooded his eyes with tears. The ashes were not just an undifferentiated fine gray power. There were shades of auburn and crimson, shards of bone stark white and brittle. He had manipulated them through the tough, slick plastic with grim fascination, hoping beyond hope that he could somehow conjure Melissa within, even more horrified that he would recognize some contour of her chin, the cusp of a tooth, a fragment from the orbits of her eyes.

But tonight he just sat on that couch and buried his face in his palms as tears rolled down. They burned and tasted extremely salty, like the alkaline wastes of a dying sea.

He stumbled to the bedroom, toppled face-first onto the flower-patterned comforter of his queen bed. The scent of her person, a lively smell that made him think of fresh-scooped melon balls for some reason, still clung faintly to the fabric. He lay motionless for hours. Sleep would not overtake him. He clenched his jaw, he balled his fists, he silently cursed the cold remorseless wastes of a universe where God was either dead or one sick cruel mother fucker. Finally he lapsed into a sort of timeless trance, a boundless blank slate of nothingness. Unremitting black and foreboding, an absence of sleep like death.

But Oliver Brinkman did not dream.

* * *

ANOTHER GRUELING DAY OF TESTS. Oliver sat in Dr. Neumann's office, this time, he was sure, for the long talk. The walls were paneled in hardwoods stained dark burgundy, the ceiling coffered with elaborate finials and moldings. The lamps were too dim, the cloud-dampened sunlight filtering past languid motes of dust too feeble to lift Oliver's mood.

Dr. Neumann slouched in a button upholstered high-backed leather chair. His elbows pivoted on the armrests, and he gestured occasionally towards a cut-away plastic model of the human brain on his glass-topped coffee table as he spoke. The plastic model's one exposed eye bulged grotesquely at Oliver; he couldn't help but glance at it again and again as Dr. Neumann spoke.

"I think I understand now what's going on," Dr. Neumann said. "The problem is what to do about it." He slouched even deeper in his chair and jounced the glass tabletop as he crossed his feet.

"It's a feedback loop. When you slip into REM sleep, the primitive deep structures of your brain—emotionally charged memories from the hypothalamus, irrepressible outpourings of anger and fear from the amygdala—constantly feed-forward vivid memories and associations of your wife... and then the augmented cognetics just as swiftly annihilate them. It's an autonomous response of self-defense. Your mind is protecting you from yourself."

"So my brain shuts down."

"In a manner of speaking. It's closer, actually, to the petit mal status that we observe in certain types of seizures... you can think of it as a sort of fibrillation of the mind. The result is that your higher brain activity is virtually undetectable while you're sleeping."

"Yet I awake unharmed."

"No. That is not correct. It's only going to get worse." Dr. Neumann took a deep breath and sighed as the distended eye of the plastic model seemed to bulge ever more grotesquely. "Without REM sleep, eventually you'll die."

"Eventually?"

"Another month or two. Maybe more, probably much less."

Oliver drew back reflexively. His mouth gaped but no sound issued forth. What could he say? Up until this moment he hadn't been sure he really wanted to keep living at all. But the sledgehammer-to-the-face reality of it derailed his dark thoughts. He imagined the relics of Melissa's doomed life scattered in the apartment, their stories forever untold, as some nameless custodian arrived to clear out the apartment for the next occupant…

Oliver tried to moisten his lips with a dried-up tongue, and swallowed hard. "Is there anything you can do to help me?"

"You have two choices. One is very bad, and the other is far worse." Dr. Neumann finally dropped his feet to the floor and leaned forward. "Tell me, Mr. Brinkman, what is it that you want out of life?"

"I just want my wife back."

"In that case I recommend radiosurgical ablation of the mammillary bodies."

"Huh?"

"Sorry." Dr. Neumann pointed his slender index finger to a wrinkled-looking lump at the very back, near the base of the plastic model's brain. "What I mean is, we'll zap this tiny little nexus of brain cells at the base of your hypothalamus. One on each side."

"And this will…?"

"It'll destroy the biological basis of memory. Suppress those latent, emotionally super-charged memories. But don't worry, your mnemonic implants will preserve the memory of your wife."

"So what's the catch?"

"I'm pretty sure it will break the deadlock, so you can sleep again, but you'll be physically incapable of forming new memories. You won't know where you are, no matter how many times someone tries to explain it to you. You won't remember if you've eaten or not. Heck, you won't remember if you need to take a dump or not. You'll need round the clock care—in a nursing home or the like. You'll basically be an invalid, but you'll be an invalid who remembers your wife."

"That sounds fucking horrible."

"All right then, forget radiosurgery. We can wipe out the aug-cogs instead. Short-circuit the mnemonics. Leave you with nothing but a primitive biological mind."

Oliver shuddered at the thought, but there was another implication that disturbed him far more deeply than having his mind revert, in essence, to that of dimly sentient beast.

"I'll forget," Oliver said, his voice barely rising above a whisper.

"Yes… In time, yes. Or perhaps immediately. It's hard to say."

"Why do you say that?"

"It's not well studied because of the ethical implications. Sudden withdrawal from cognitive enhancements can be disastrous… it might kill you faster than the insomnia. Or if it doesn't, you might wish it had."

"So let me get this straight. You can destroy my mind, and I'll be a walking zombie locked in a vivid state of perpetual grief." Oliver wiped the film of cold sweat from his brow. "Or you can wipe out the electro-mnemonics and eradicate the memory of my wife—kill her again, in other words—and I'll either die or wish I was dead. And no matter what I choose, it might not work."

"That's pretty much it."

* * *

ANOTHER NIGHT, ANOTHER LONG AIMLESS drive, another cold front blowing through the perpetual gloam of the Seattle skyline.

Oliver stepped into his apartment, drenched by the brief dash from the carport to the door. He plopped down into the deep-seated impression of himself in the white-and-gray striped couch cushion. It was a depression that would only grow deeper with time, as if his fate had already been decided by a past self that foreshadowed his every move.

He cupped his forehead in his hands and in the incessant darkness of his mind he inventoried Melissa's possessions, the dusty relics of his grief, yet again. The hairbrush. The unfinished book of love stories. The white emergency candles. The bicycle helmet. The vacuum. The ornate rosewood box.

What was the cipher concealed among these monuments of the banal and exquisite melancholy alike, what unspoken testament of Melissa's life awaited within them?

Lightning flashed. The heavens cracked asunder and came crashing back together.

Oliver's apartment went dark.

But a brilliant nova of divine inspiration exploded within his mind.

By memory he crept through the blackout to the table. He fumbled for the emergency candles, the box of matches nearby.

He lit a candle and clutched it, a tiny beacon of light in the pitch blackness, as he gathered what he needed.

He pulled a hacksaw from his toolbox and sawed a length of hose from the vacuum cleaner. He retrieved two fresh vacuum-cleaner bags from the closet.

He combed the loose strands of Melissa's auburn hair from her brush on the vanity.

He picked up the book of love stories, pages still averted from his eyes, and held it overhead, arms outstretched, as if he were revealing the holy word to an invisible congregation.

He gathered together other items as well. Wire strippers and lengths of copper speaker wire. A few items of Melissa's clothing. Armrests that he unscrewed from her tilt/swivel chair in the improvised office of the tiny guest bedroom. Chair legs that he pried loose from the laminated birch dining-table chairs they'd received as a wedding gift.

Oliver set to work. Through the night he sawed and he stripped wires and he bound objects together. When one candle dimmed he lit another. To the exterior he affixed the armrests and the chair legs. He mounted the bicycle helmet on top. He exhaled sharply into the vacuum cleaner bags to inflate them, and then these too he fastened in place. He split one end of the sawed-off vacuum-cleaner hose and duct-taped it, so that it forked into to each bag. Behind the smaller of these he tucked the book of love stories, still open to the fateful page that separated the life Melissa had lived from the life that could have been.

At the break of dawn, when he had finished, Oliver retrieved one last thing.

He lifted the heavy plastic bag from the Brazilian rosewood box.

With a box-knife he slashed away the knot sealing the bag shut.

He held the neck of the plastic bag below the bicycle helmet, and poured the ashes into the throat of the vacuum-cleaner hose.

Oliver Brinkman infused what he had assembled, the cobbled-together idol-effigy of his dead wife, with the last remaining cinders of her departed soul. Fine filaments of powder rose up and licked at the air, the tang of potash scratched at his throat.

But for some reason it evoked the scent of fresh-scooped melon balls.

When the last of the dust settled, he kissed her. No lightning flashed, but a jolt of energy burst through him nonetheless.

Her neck listed slightly. Though he held no match to them, the wicks of her white emergency-candle eyes danced with flame again. Her windpipe, the sawed off length of vacuum hose, hissed with a single breath, and then after a long pause, another. And another.

"I am so tired, my love," Oliver said. "It is time we lay us down to sleep."

He lifted the effigy of his wife in his arms and walked to the bedroom. He settled her makeshift body under the covers. He rested his weary head upon his own pillow, next to hers, and gazed forlornly into the dimly flickering flames of her eyes.

From her ashes, Oliver had conjured Melissa. She had arisen.

And when he kissed her a second time, something shorted out in his mind.

He closed his eyes, and sleep soon overtook him. He thought he heard a heartbeat of sorts, a sound not unlike someone thumbing through the pages of a hardcover-bound book. He imagined a voice that whispered his name in the dark. He had the distinct phantom sensation of warm, supple lips that met his own when he whispered her name in return.

He had finally removed the relics of her life from their long-frozen stasis. He had shepherded her life force along, and with it followed his own—on a new path, a new way forward, a fresh vision of the future.

He let grief end, and finally allowed true remembrance—an honest, respectful forgetting embarked upon with undying love—to work its way through his mind. He was no longer a man dead inside.

Oliver Brinkman dreamed.

2

BILKING TIME

"TIME TRAVEL?" I SHOUTED, INCREDULOUS. The echoes of my voice reverberated from the rafters of Memorial Gymnasium like the doubts of a former self—the one-time Dr. Antoine Beasley of paltry *untenured* assistant professor status. But I'd risen far beyond that. "Cramer, you're a bloody fool. If the department chair gets wind of this..."

My three-point attempt clanged off the front rim and bounded over the backboard, as if to emphasize the ludicrousness of his proposal.

"No, that's not what I said." Cramer's left dimple ticced, as it always did when he became agitated. "Not time travel. I, myself, prefer the phrase 'quantum retroactive causality.' They're completely different varmints." Cramer dwelled on the word—*vaaaar-mints*—with his characteristic Yankee drawl, and retrieved the basketball. He dribbled to the corner, staying a full stride below the baseline. I knew what was coming—damn Cramer and his over-the-backboard shot—another trick from his seemingly bottomless bag of impossibilities.

"I don't know what sort of 'var-mint' you're talking about, but I smell a rat. A big, fat, snaggle-toothed black sewer rat to be exact. If what you say were true, once I received the message I'd simply decide not to send it to myself and then—Poof! I'd bilk the message—and probably my sanity along with it—out of existence. It's simply impossible."

Swish. Cramer's high-arcing shot splashed through the twine without so much as grazing the rim.

"Bah. Time is nothing but a shadowplay, a statistical aberration of quantum thermodynamics. Hasn't it ever occurred to you, Beasley, that the entire web of certainty we've laid out for ourselves is strung just a little bit too taut? While at the same time the glaring obviousness of our stupidity swills all around us? We have two 'perfect' theories of reality"—by this he meant the mutually incompatible theories of the quantum and of relativity—"while at the same time we've come to realize that we have absolutely no idea what makes up some ninety-six percent of the observable universe. Not to mention that which is patently unobservable."

My attempt to repeat his shot caromed wildly off the corner of the backboard. That made H-O-R-S for me. Dammit, Cramer was twelve years my senior, pushing the downhill side of fifty, and he was going to beat me *again*.

And to make the barb all the thornier in my side, he had a point.

Dark matter, dark energy, and the all-pervasive arrow of time. Vast blank continents of ignorance, marked only "Here be dragons."

Yes, my colleague and erstwhile HORSE rival had a point. An utterly unpublishable, scientifically untenable, and conspicuously ill-funded point, but a point nonetheless.

Cramer tried his over-the-backboard shot again, but it rimmed out. Perhaps it was my lucky day after all.

It was hard to ignore that gleam in his eyes. Damned hard. But I sure as hell was going to try. I turned my back on him and dribbled out well past the three-point line. "Why should I help you?" I asked him—darn near yelled.

The courts were deserted at 6:15 A.M. and I knew perfectly well he could hear me just fine. Next he'd awkwardly bring up the idea of a joint proposal yet again, and to tell the truth I was getting more than a little weary of my once-inimitable elder riding on my coattails.

I launched a thirty-five footer, the extreme limit of my range, and nailed the bastard wouldn'tcha know. *Match that, J. Peabody Cramer, Ph. D., Full Professor of Hassatuxet University and Perlmutter Chair of Theoretical Physics.*

But for once Cramer surprised me.

"Just because the universe doesn't make it easy for us to peer beneath the water doesn't mean there aren't leviathans stirring in the deep."

And wouldn't you know but his heave rattled home. I had nothing in my arsenal he couldn't match.

"All right, you win. I've got thirty-K earmarked for a Chinese post-doc who can't get his visa approved before the fiscal year runs out. I'll lose the money if I don't spend it—so it's yours if you don't make me collect that final E."

"Deal," he said. But as we departed he couldn't resist a final rainbow jumper—launched below the baseline and past the out-of-bounds stripe of the far corner—*Swish*. Just to show me up, just to prove he would've won anyway.

Quantum retrocausality my ass. I swear, he's fitted all these basketballs with electromagnets. Something that lets him engage in this spooky action at a distance.

The thought that he's not cheating, that he really is just that plain good at his game, is a possibility too terrible to contemplate.

So I did what any sensible scientist would do: I showered up, went to my office, and solved the problem by not thinking about it.

And my solution, such as it was, worked pretty damn good for another eleven days.

* * *

I CAME ACROSS WIGDOR LATE ON A FRIDAY evening, in the deserted shoals of Gentry Hall, home of the Hassatuxet University Physics Department. The dark-stained oak doors of the other professors—Associate, Full, and Chaired alike—had long since been closed and locked for the weekend, casting a preternatural twilight over the long hallway. But one door, Dr. Dennison Wigdor's, cast a jaundiced shaft from his lone desk lamp, attesting to his lowly untenured status of Assistant Professor.

Most junior faculty fail to appreciate the fine art of the backhanded compliment, so every so often I take it upon myself to further their education.

"Wigdor!" I interjected loudly—too loudly—and he flinched at his keyboard. "That poster your post-doc just had accepted is damned fine work—very fine indeed!"

Now to tell you the truth I knew nothing about the work. But I didn't have to in order to whiff the reek of failure wafting about it. Poster, as you may well appreciate, is code for *not a proper scientific paper*. As in, work that has not been accepted for oral presentation at a scientific symposium. As in, work relegated to an ill-attended poster session, in direct opposition to talks by esteemed luminaries of the field, and a perfectly respectable backwater for uninspired research efforts to saunter off and die.

Only this time I was wrong. Damned wrong, and Cramer—through Wigdor, his heir-apparent and closest ally on the Physics Department faculty—was about to hand me my ass in a basket yet again.

"Did I show you the reviews?" Wigdor asked, scrabbling at his brow as if to rid it of some infestation. "One referee gave the original paper a ten out of ten, saying it was a breakthrough of the first order. A second said that it was flat-out wrong—a work of sheer fantasy—and gave it a one. The third—anonymous, of course, but who claimed he was a Nobel laureate—stated the proof was a tautological exercise in self-flagellation with the conclusion built into the assumptions, and rated it a zero. The associate editor said it 'showed promise' and 'might provoke discussion'—code for 'not convincing' and 'likely to inspire ridicule'—and forwarded it to the posters chair for consideration. She ultimately accepted it, but under the condition that we were to 'tone down our claims regarding the thermodynamic properties of spacetime' and that we remove our speculations regarding the 'imaginary-time interpretation of Maxwell's equations.'

Wigdor was referring to the equations governing the behavior of electromagnetic fields—the enigmatic zephyr of light itself. And of course, if one replaced the real-numbered time variable t with an imaginary number, then the equations remained completely valid—in negative energy, imaginary time, and other such fantastical constructions.

All was possible so long as cause and effect remained entangled in their twin destinies.

So when Wigdor embarked upon this foolish opening, I immediately seized the opportunity to twist the knife of my whimsical scorn.

"Ah yes—a fine afternoon exercise for an undergraduate thesis, a pedestrian stroll through second-order differential equations--" here I rubbed my stubble as if I needed to wipe the dripping sarcasm from my chin—"though I must confess I'm a bit surprised you hadn't bothered to chart out more challenging terrain for your post-doc, if he's such a promising young protégé?"

But instead of retreating, Wigdor just smirked.

"You haven't actually bothered to look at the poster, have you?"

"Of course not. Such trifles--"

He leaned over and pulled out a large foam-core panel from behind his desk.

The headline got my attention pretty well:

TIME DOES NOT EXIST.

* * *

I FOLLOWED WIGDOR TO THE PHOTONICS LAB, a drab twenty-by-thirty chamber of taupe-painted cinderblock in the basement. An optical bench dominated the room; a miniaturized cityscape of a misbegotten technological future-*extremis* festooned the rectangular grid of perforations in the bench's stainless steel slab. Laser sources, crystals, half-silvered mirrors, and all other manner of strange contrivances.

But what really caught my eye were the enormous spools of ultra-lossless fiber-optic cable in the corner.

"Let me show you," Wigdor said.

He fired up the laser and a pair of nondescript white blobs appeared on a computer screen.

"The beam enters the crystal and exits as quantum-entangled photon pairs. These arrive at a foil, pierced by a double slit, then pass through to a detector plate, which records where each photon strikes."

"Your standard double-slit experiment," I said. "Just switch the detector position to double the focal length and you'll have your pretty little interference pattern."

"Of course." Wigdor seemed suddenly emboldened as he crossed his arms in front of his broad chest. "You do seem to have a penchant for stating the obvious—you've been working on a lecture for your undergraduate course, no?"

I ground my teeth, but didn't take the bait.

"Perhaps you failed to note this," Wigdor said, waving his hand at one of the half-silvered mirrors. "Half the photons reflect from the mirror, the other half pass through. One entangled pair, two different paths. The first leads to the double slit apparatus, but not until—" he pointed to the fiber-optic spools and vigorously spiraled his finger in the air "—it completes a tightly-wound hundred-kilometer detour. Meanwhile, the other photon—having passed through the mirror unhindered—has already struck a secondary detector."

My jaw unhinged itself. The flash of insight Wigdor had been steering me towards the entire time finally struck me. "And because the photons are entangled," I said, "the secondary detector also shows the interference pattern—or not—"

The implications were mind-blowing—I couldn't finish the thought. So instead my hands came unbidden to my temples and seized fistfuls of hair, tiny insane brooms that thrust through my fingers.

"That's right," Wigdor said. "The correct and corresponding pattern appears on the secondary detector, *five milliseconds before we decide the focal length of the main detector.* Even though those photons took an independent path—even though they never passed through a double-slit—even though they completed their journey long before their quantum-entangled twins encountered their double-slit dilemma!"

"So you've demonstrated nonlocal signaling," I said, "with a message that arrives before you sent it."

"Yes." Wigdor licked his lips; he suddenly looked nervous again. "We believe so."

"I have but one question," I said, and paused for effect. It was time to turn this whole little foray back to my advantage.

"What happens if you detect the message—and then decide not to send it?"

The Bilking Paradox. Now I had him. I'd trapped him in a logical fallacy. It was a contradiction—you couldn't receive a message you didn't send, and yet the purported message from the future had already arrived.

Did I mention quantum paradoxes give me a headache?

"We already tried that." Wigdor's expression turned sour. "You're not going to like the result."

"How do you mean?"

"Care to try it yourself?"

* * *

THE COMPUTER SCREEN SHOWED a steady interference pattern, venetian-blind bands of light that faded towards the fringes. It was the classic demonstration of light's wave-like manifestation, where the expanding ripple of a photon's wave function interfered with itself.

I keyed in my message at the prompt.

>>> HELLO THERE.

A rapid-fire burst of interference bands flickered on the display. A squarewave marched across the computer screen, rising and falling edges etching out the bit-code of my banal shout into the quantum void.

"Now let's try that again," Wigdor said, "but this time we'll program the computer to wait for a rising edge, and then we'll cancel the message transmission as soon as we receive it."

An interference pattern, steady and resolute, stared back at me like some mysterious one-eyed quantum insect.

Nothing changing, no message.

"Okay... nothing. Extremely impressive." I'd let the sarcasm, that air of superiority, drip back into my voice even though Wigdor had me highly engaged at this point.

"Not quite, Your Excellency. You forgot to tap 'Go.'"

Of course. The big green button. I'd been so focused on the interference pattern that I'd totally failed to perceive the large green button's existence.

I reached out, hand trembling, and pressed my fingertip to the touch-screen.

Another frenetic burst of waveforms squiggled across the screen.

"I don't get it. It's the same as before."

"No." Wigdor pointed to an inset on a second monitor with the message squarewaves fixed in place, one directly above the other. "Look more closely."

I leaned forward, squinted my eyes. The squarewaves looked similar, but the edges didn't match up.

They were different. And the second, I now saw, was much longer.

More bits.

"We sent a different message?"

"No. You sent—in the future—the exact same message and then decided—in the past—not to send it."

"So what's this long message?"

Now Wigdor pointed a thick, meaty finger at what looked like a chat window. It contained the message history of the transmitted bit-codes.

>>> HELLO THERE

(message received; transmission successful)

>>> HELLO THERE

(user error, causality violation: message bilked)

<<< KNOCK IT OFF YOU BLOODY FOOL. DO YOU HAVE ANY IDEA OF THE HAVOC YOU ARE WREAKING OVER HERE

(end of message)

"What is that?" I said. "Who keyed that in?"

"I don't know," said Wigdor. Perhaps it's you. Perhaps it's me. It could be my post-doc. Or maybe it's Cramer. Somebody—it could be almost anyone really—in the future."

"But nobody's here typing a different message. That time is long since come and gone. Five milliseconds is five milliseconds."

"Is it? It is really?"

"Of course."

"What if we were to replace that spool with a resonant optical cavity?"

"So you can store a reflecting photon more or less indefinitely. Whoop-de-doo, hooray for you."

"And we launched it into orbit?"

"Let me guess. Resonant Photons IN SPACE… the title of your latest space opera pulp novel?"

"For exactly one full year," Wigdor said. "Traveling, of course, at an extremely high velocity while its entangled twin awaits, dormant, here within Earth's inertial rest frame…"

"My God," I said. "If you leave it up there long enough—or if the spacecraft reaches a significant fraction of the speed of light--"

"We can extend quantum retrocausality as far into the past as we like."

"I'll help you write the grant. When can we submit a proposal? How soon can we requisition a satellite launch window?"

"Twenty-three months ago. We've already done it. The spool in the corner is just for show; it's not actually hooked up to anything any longer."

I stamped my feet, I slapped my cheeks. This was it—exultant majesty—a sublime revelation. Such moments come once in a career, once in a lifetime. "Your post-doc. What's his name again? He's a genius—you're a genius—by God, this will get us a Nobel Prize!"

"Get 'us' a Nobel prize, my erstwhile colleague? I think, of ego, His Excellency doth possess too much."

"I can help—I mean I can fill in the theoretical--"

Wigdor just shook his head, a smirk on his lips. "My post-doc's name is James, by the way. James Peabody Cramer. I believe you enjoy playing HORSE with him during your morning workout? He'll make a fine faculty member one day."

*　*　*

OF COURSE, IT WASN'T ACTUALLY CRAMER who was Wigdor's post-doc. Not exactly, anyway. A younger, kinder, and eminently sharper version of Cramer who went by the pseudonym of Wesley Kirkpatrick.

But it was him all right. I was certain of it the first morning he joined Cramer and I at our daily

HORSE grudge-match. The mannerisms, the same tic of the left cheek, the same Yankee drawl to his pronouncements.

And that same high-arcing over-the-backboard jump shot, God damn his entangled souls—both of them.

I was already at H-O-R-S and seriously considering a half-court heave as my attempt, improbable though it was, because it was about the only shot I might make that neither Cramer (he of hypothetical retirement age) nor "Kirkpatrick" (the J. Peabody Cramer of three decades past) could match.

But just as I drew the basketball with both hands to my chest, Kirkpatrick's friend walked in, a young fella with a wiry pelt of black hair, dribbling a basketball between his legs as he approached us. He pounded the ball against the floor with confidence, the steady thump-thump-thump reverberating from the rafters of the gymnasium like my own confidence of old. I, too, had been a good ball-handler once, but that had been a long, long time ago.

I drifted in from half-court to meet him, but he eluded my handshake. I awkwardly redirected my hand, and instead ran my fingers through my own sweaty but wire-brush stiff salt-and-pepper gray hair.

"Hello there," he said, looking me right in the eye. He pivoted at thirty-five feet and launched a majestic over-the shoulder jump shot, with perfect backspin that kissed the twine and sent the ball rolling right back to him once it hit the hardwood.

"Or should I say," he said, taking a deep breath so that he could enunciate his next words— "HELLO THERE."

The man's deep voice echoed back from the rafters.

For the second time in as many days, my jaw gaped wide. Sad to say—but I must admit—I believe this time I actually did drool on myself.

For now I had to face—I had to match, shot for shot, letter for letter, epiphany for epiphany— not only Cramer and "Kirkpatrick," but also this athletic young man—my former future self—the man I'd bilked on the Cramer Ansible, as I have since dubbed our ungodly apparatus.

For, as Einstein would have it, God doesn't play dice.

But he might just play H-O-R-S-E, and while the dude can do a great many things—small miracles, the world in seven days, and all that—he sure as hell can't make a goddamned thirty-five foot jump shot.

I tried to match my former self, clanged it up and over the backboard yet again. Cramer missed. Kirkpatrick missed. We all acquired that dreaded final E.

I'd lost. And I'd won. A little of both, a little of neither. Me and my new protégé will do (have done) great things. Maybe even beat out Cramer (and Kirkpatrick (and Wigdor)). I just hope they don't have more help on the way. I've already asked for more, myself—I think. It's so hard to keep track of things these days. My memory is not quite what it used to be.

Or perhaps it is, and I've bilked myself yet again.

Hello there. Hello there yet again. HELLO THERE indeed.

I couldn't resist slipping back into the lab afterwards for one final bit of quantum frivolity.

>>> HAVE YOU, PERCHANCE, BEEN PRAC-TICING YOUR OVER-THE-BACKBOARD SHOT?

(message received; transmission successful)

<<< NO. JUST BILKING TIME OVER HERE. CRAMER SENDS HIS REGARDS TO WIGDOR, BTW.

YOU, ON THE OTHER HAND, CAN GO TO H-E-L-L.

(end of message)

Oh well. Can't win 'em all. And that may be right where I'm headed.

But at least it doesn't spell H-O-R-S-E.

Goddamned Wigdor. Goddamned "post-doc." Goddamned Cramer and his double-slit over-the-backboard shots.

He's playing God now, I'm afraid, and the dice are quite loaded.

3

GREAT
RED

ONE

THE EYEWALL CLEAVED THE SKY from horizon to horizon in a ragged crimson gash. Vast webs of lightning electrocuted the bruised and bloodied cloudscape. Vermillion anvils towered like malevolent gods over the colossal maw of the anti-cyclone, Jovian demons ravening to smash worlds and devour continents. High above the three-man, herringboned cirrus clouds caged the yawning black cadaver of space as the largest storm in the Solar System sundered them to flailing white rags of ammonia-ice.

Piotr Petschnigg flinched and averted his eyes with a sour expression even as he committed the craft to its final plunge, not because he was terrified or squeamish or so much as having second thoughts, but because the utterly alien and remorseless panorama captured something within him more perfectly than he could have imagined possible.

His solar plexus churned in slow-motion synchrony with the tempest. He set his canines hard against one another and his lips curled ever so slightly in a pantomime of the primal snarl as he leaned into the yoke. The temperature was still a hundred Centigrade below zero and the pressure was no more than the whisper of a dying brother's breath in his ear but both of these dimensions would soon bear down on the quantum-sintered graphene hull of the *Mother May I* with more pressure than a man's mind could bear.

Why was he here in this jury-rigged watermelon seed of a spaceship that stank of scorched plastic and mildewed sweat? Every time he breathed, the air tasted like a burnt microwave lasagna tray. Sure, nobody had ever been nuts enough to try this before—this was the Last of the Great

Firsts, as Francois liked to brag—but wasn't there something more productive they could do with their lives than toss them into the implacable roiling bowels of Jupiter?

Perhaps, perhaps not. Something drove him. Something drove all of them. It was a feeling inside that he could never stop running, that he was falling all the time, that the world reeled beneath his feet every time he took a step. Maybe it didn't matter and this insatiable drive was simply hardwired into certain defective manifestations of mankind. People like himself and Francois and Amalthea. People with deep psychic trauma beyond the reach of science and communion alike, or with just plain bad wiring in some critical neuronal junction. An all-consuming desire to ascend to the ultimate summits and to delve into the deepest abysses and to behold whatever vista lay beyond the final foothills of reason.

No matter the cost—to life, to love, to sanity.

As if, Piotr thought, such a conquest—such a foolish errand—could fill the boundless dark vortex ever lurking beneath the surface of his skin.

Maybe he just had to know. What drove the immortal howling engine of the Great Red Spot.

What mysteries lurked below the seething seas of hydride slush, long hypothesized but never witnessed. Whether one could dredge a sample of the fabled metallic hydrogen shimmering in the vast hell-forges of Jupiter, raise it to the cloud tops, return it at an escape velocity of 215,000 kilometers an hour to the scrutiny of science and inter-planetary renown.

If he survived to tell the tale, all the better. But either way, he'd have himself an Epic.

Piotr remembered that crisp April dawn he'd summited K2 with Amalthea. Atop her lean hot-pink snowsuit, her oxygen mask—half-mirrored polycarbonate black as a wasp's eye—gave her an alien appearance and reflected only his own fun-house visage against the near-pornographic heliotrope of snow-pinnacled summits that serrated the horizon. *Getting to the top is the easy part,* she'd said.

Same was true, he suspected, of the Great Red Spot of Jupiter.

There was only one direction to go from here, and from the top of this great swirling son of a bitch, it was one hell of a long way down.

TWO

THE PALLID RAYS OF A SUN nearly a billion kilometers distant filtered through specters of gilded mist. Phantom landforms billowed from the cloud deck in the great battlements and parapets of a dizzying aerie cast in ocher haze, a vision of a fabled Jovian realm that had appeared before Piotr's eyes and then somehow failed to fully materialize.

He angled the craft lower.

The jets outside the hull roared past at over 330 kilometers per hour and the atmosphere had not quite reached ten bars, but already the titanium spars popped and cracked with the pressure.

If not for the quantum counter-pressure fields permeating the hull, the ship and all three of its passengers would already be smashed flatter than a cockroach caught out at high noon in Brooklyn.

The superconductive shell deflected the worst of the radiation and Jupiter's intense magnetic field, but still Piotr's fillings tasted like he'd bitten into a gigantic buzzing wad of aluminum foil.

Piotr could hear Francois fumbling with the crates in the back, obsessively organizing and re-organizing the instruments and spare parts and such victuals as they possessed.

Forget about the core of Jupiter. If he could stuff a balloon up Francois' arse they'd have an ingot of the fabled metallic hydrogen in ten seconds flat. What Amalthea saw in him Piotr had no idea.

Piotr caught the light citrus scent of her skin, but still he flinched at the warm, delicate press of her hand on his shoulder.

"Piotr." Blades of Amalthea's long straight hair, black and glossy as anthracite, hung over her crevasse-blue eyes.

A rare chance for a private conversation. As private as it got, at least, on a glorified parade float with barely a hundred cubic meters between them.

But he couldn't think of a single word to say to her.

Not. One. Word.

Always the conversationalist, that was him. Jeesh.

As the awkward pause stretched to eternity she finally, mercifully, continued. "I have to admit—I'm terrified. Any sign of turbulence yet?"

Piotr glanced at his instruments. "Not yet. Soon. Better take your Dramamine."

"Ha ha. Aren't you worried, though?"

"Nah. I duct-taped this heap of remanufactured plastic together myself. It's the best money can buy."

"Yeah, if you're an unemployed ice-hound from Ceres."

"I prefer to say *experienced*, myself. And I didn't say how much money."

Amalthea smiled, but then she glanced down and her lips slipped sideways into a half-grimace. "Don't tell Francois I said this, but I'm having second thoughts. I have no idea what the hell I'm doing here."

The ship trembled as it passed through a diaphanous white curtain. The wind hissed past and peppered the hull with the rapid-fire tick, tick, ticking of tiny ice crystals.

Piotr thrust a finger past Amalthea, pointed out the viewscreen. "Well I'll be damned."

Amalthea turned and looked with him. Immense glittering arcs emblazoned the horizon, linking a half dozen mock suns into brilliant fleur-de-lises of pale yellow sunbursts. Sublime double-rainbows encircled the heavens and joined the sun dogs in a spectral globe, as if the cloud tops were haunted by the wayward proto-planets that Jupiter had devoured in its remote youth.

"Ah, my love. If I didn't have such a way with words, I'd tell you it's more beautiful than you are." Piotr winked at Amalthea and smiled, but she didn't meet his eye.

Her jaw hung slack in wonder, her teeth shining like pale white lanterns in the mysterious deep of her soul.

Piotr licked his lips and gestured again at the vast spectacle outside. "But instead I guess I'll just tell you: that might be your answer right there."

THREE

THE RUDDY MIST HISSED past the black-silk hull at a steady five hundred and ten kilometers an hour. Streamers of muted yellows and pale cobalt blues braided themselves into the jets like darting snakes. The ship raced towards a far-off gradient of deep dusky browns, raw siennas, and burnt umbers that never seemed to draw closer and barely distinguished one quadrant of the unworldly sky from another.

The ship dropped lower, through another of the endless strata of hazes, and began to shake.

The hissing rose in a mighty crescendo as the mist paled into a pure virginal white. Shear instabilities growled and shrieked at the hull like the ragged throat of a decapitated monster that would inhale the world.

Then the clouds broke and the horizon rushed at the windscreen in vivid scarlet streaks that ran like blood and Piotr remembered the night he'd left the fate of his brother to the mountain.

* * *

DENALI, THE TALLEST PEAK IN NORTH AMERICA. Winter.

Two men.

One ascent.

No line of retreat.

They huddled in the unrelenting bore of the jet stream, screaming blitzkrieg gusts that assailed them with salvos of wind-lashed snow and tiny bayonets of ice.

They were caught out of the tent, no going up, no turning back.

They'd pitched the cramped blue-nylon temple that would be their salvation, if only they could find it, at the fifty-eight hundred meter level of Denali. Made a final push for the summit, only to be beaten back by a tempest that threatened to blow them right off their feet and over the sheer three thousand foot black-pinnacled drop to the glacier far below.

The white-out left them utterly directionless. Lost.

Piotr shortened the eight-millimeter nylon lifeline tying him to Gunther, picked a direction heading vaguely downslope, and prayed to God it was the right one.

My some miracle Gunther stumbled across the tent. Piotr had missed it, and was about to plunge right off the cornice overhanging the cliff face when Gunther pulled the rope taut.

One more step and Piotr would have stepped into empty space and ripped Gunther off the mountain with him.

They hunkered down in the cramped blue nylon tent, boiling water for lemonade, with a pinch of melted chocolate. They tried to pound some feeling back into their hands and feet before frostbite ceded the first parcels of flesh to the frozen corpses their bodies yearned to become.

"What should we start with when we return to civilization?"

"How about a pepperoni pizza?" Gunther ventured. He'd taken quite a liking to American food. "With extra cheese."

"Deep pan!"

"And sausage and bacon and meat."

"Yes, meat! More meat."

"And anchovies."

"I hate anchovies! But why the hell not. Anchovies are meat and meat is good."

"Anchovies it is!"

"And a fine young Alaskan maiden to warm our beds!"

"Ah Gunther, watch out for those Alaskan girls." Piotr combed his fingernails through his unkempt beard. "I hear they're hairier than an East German grizzly."

"There's no grizzlies in East Germany."

"And there's no fine young maidens in Alaska."

"All right then, forget the maidens. Make that a stein full of *doppel bock*, and a keg with no bottom!"

They laughed and Piotr watched their breath plume to the ceiling of the tent and freeze instantly into wisps of white frost on the blue fabric trembling in the wind.

Their conversation seemed to freeze with it.

They waited. They listened to the tent nylon chatter and snap in the storm. They refused to pray because to do so would be to admit that their fate did not rest in their own hands.

At as the hours dragged on Piotr slipped into a shallow, fitful slumber. A vision of the girl that had caught his fancy in the Karakoram shimmered in the verdant sawgrass of a meadow, her thick jet-black hair hanging over her face like the inverted spires of some forbidden and unattainable black-rock peak that loomed high overhead.

She brushed her hair from the glacier-blue seracs of her eyes and at the moment he got a good look at her—*into her*—for the first time, the ice shattered and her face sheared off, a great tumult of ice and stone roaring down the mountain, directly towards him and Gunther and—

Piotr jerked upright at the eerie booming shotgun-crack that echoed through the darkness. The report lingered in the air, began to build, gathered fury as it roiled down the mountain.

A vast avalanche slab had broken loose somewhere high above, and the sole question now was what lay in its path.

And whether they would be alive thirty seconds from now to find out.

* * *

THE SNOWPACK SHUDDERED BENEATH PIOTR'S sleeping pad. The white death rumbled closer, ever louder and more violent, until he knew no other sound. Soon it would pass or they'd be dead. He screamed out his brother's name, or thought he did, but it was hard to separate the impulses coursing through his mind from reality.

And then everything crushed in on him and he had the sensation of tumbling like a rag doll and fine crystals of snow melted and froze instantly under his coat, into his trousers, down his windpipe.

The world stopped.

Piotr's universe was hard-packed snow and silence and darkness.

He felt his heart beating wildly in his chest. He had not even the sensation of ribs or arms or legs or a face. A hard rubbery numbness crept up through his flesh and into his soul.

He had to breathe or he'd be dead in a minute. Two minutes top.

Piotr heard furious clawing above his head, muffled shouts, the dim glow of a headlamp, and finally a distinct wet *thop* that he'd never forget as the cork of hardened snow popped out of his throat.

Then the sound of his own gasps and Gunther sobbing his name, over and over again.

He was free, and would soon wish he were dead.

* * *

SOMEHOW GUNTHER'S SIDE OF THE TENT had remained anchored to the slope. Another couple of feet and the avalanche would have swept them away entirely. Piotr had lost his pack and his sleeping pad, but fortunately he'd already been wearing every stitch of clothing he'd brought with him and he'd stashed his boots over on Gunther's side, by the entrance to the tent.

Gunther turned off his headlamp to save the battery. Piotr huddled against his brother in the darkness, embracing him in a shameless way that they probably hadn't shared in decades, as they both shivered and waited for dawn to break.

Gunter leaned towards him even as the gale intensified and shrieked, cupped his hands to Piotr's ear, tried to shout something.

Piotr shouted back *What?* and the second avalanche hit. Almost soundless this time, a hissing serpent of snow that wrapped itself deeper and deeper around their bodies. Piotr hugged Gunther to his chest with all his strength, fisted his brother's down parka with hands clamped like frozen vices of flesh. Yet still—it couldn't have taken more than a few seconds, but seemed to last for long-drawn minutes—Gunther pulled away, and though Piotr could see nothing in the abject darkness, afterwards he always imagined Gunther looking back at him, eyes wide and round, mouth gaping wordlessly as the avalanche dragged him over the precipice and away into the eternal black abyss.

When dawn broke Piotr sat, still buried to his chest in the snow. Tears leaked from his eyes, frozen in an archipelago of icy dollops on the ruddy crimson carapace of his cheeks.

Gunther was gone.

And in the end, after the funeral without a body and having to explain what'd happened to their mother over and over again and the interminable sleepless nights and the weeks and months and years of suffering and grieving, one thing remained that haunted Piotr Petschnigg more than anything else.

Over the soulless mind-rending shrieks of the

storm, he hadn't been able to hear the last words that Gunther had ever spoken.

FOUR

THREE-QUARTERS OF A BILLION KILOMETERS AWAY and plunged in the thick of a mere four and a half hours of darkness, Piotr Petschnigg struggled to endure the second-longest night he had ever known.

Sour bile shot up his throat and the blood drained from his head as the ship plummeted into yet another savage downdraft. He steeled his shoulders and bore his feet into the floor to hold the controls steady. Six hundred and sixty kilometer-per-hour jets screamed past the hull, but somehow it failed to disintegrate once again. He'd built her good and Francois' calculations had been true.

Either that or they were all about to die.

Piotr took a deep draught of the stale, dank air to try and keep the puke at bay a bit longer. That was when he caught the scent again. That delicate citrus smell.

Couldn't turn and look now, not with Francois sitting right next to him and everything but his left nut bolted down in this goddamned seven-point harness.

But that soothing citrus smell and the thought of the tender inverted crescent curve that Amalthea's nose made when he caught her profile at the right angle calmed his stomach and brought his mind back into focus. Only took a second or two. Funny how that worked.

Meanwhile Francois manipulated the sensor arrays and tried to sniff out the neutrino band. Something to tell them where they were, something to help map out the ever-shifting terrain ahead, something to give them a clue where to go.

Piotr could see his friend's reflection in the glossy instrument panels, his clean-shaven jaw, his sharp-angled nose—broken several times in exactly that way that men would say gave him character and women would say made him sexy—and most of all those penetrating brown eyes.

"Still nothing? C'mon, man, don't make me come over there."

"Go ahead, keep manhandling your ugly Bavarian girl-friend." Francois fingered the trackpad, trying to will the signal's ghost-particles to materialize on his screen. "This mademoiselle over here, she requires the gentleman's touch."

Piotr just prayed Francois found something—a calm, an eddy, even a jet a little less violent—and found it damned quick.

He could see almost nothing in the murk now.

Deep crimson phantoms loomed and shot past the ship, bumps and dips and shudders knocked at the hull and shook the loose panels and jiggled the cargo with a constant high-frequency squeaking that wouldn't go away except when they hit the big drops.

A sudden squall of hail drummed against the ship, a frenzied rhythm that knew no human logic. Knocks and thuds. Louder. Again and again. A distant sustained flickering went off, an apparition of white light veiled by the clouds, followed by a long rumbling crescendo of thunder.

Then a gigantic flash close by.

The brilliant stroke of lightning strobed the grotesqueries of mist, flash-frozen white serpents coiling through fantastical tottering badlands of cloud.

Piotr felt like he was being mashed down in his seat and the tone of the hiss outside shifted down a register and he had the distinct sensation that the ship was accelerating down a steep ramp.

The ship hit the end and dropped.

A tremendous thunderclap pummeled the transport with the fury of a colossus, made the spars screech like nails pulled from a freshly-sealed coffin. His teeth rattled and his spleen shook with a disquieting low-frequency vibration. The wind gathered itself, the gusts congregated and bayed like depraved wolf-gods in the distance.

Piotr wrestled with the controls and tried to find his own calm in the trembling needles and dials of the instruments, but there was none to be had. The altimeter spun in a senseless blur and the anemometer was pegged to its ceiling and his horizon indicator was barely five degrees from the level even though he could swear it felt like the ship was diving and banking hard left.

He couldn't give in to that fear, he couldn't give in to those phantom sensations. *Trust your instruments, always your instruments.*

And the instruments said the ship was fine, attitude normal. But they had to get the hell out of this turbulence. *Which way to go?*

Francois snapped his fingers and pointed at the screen. "Got it!"

"Give me a bearing!"

The ship chattered and shook as if it were being wrung across an enormous washboard. Jets shrieked and hissed as they sheared past the hull. The sensation of vertigo began to take hold, an anti-cyclone rapidly spiraling out of control.

"Here. An eddy." Francois pointed at a void in the specks of light dotting his screen. "And it looks like it connects to a deep convection cylinder."

"Which way?"

"Down and hard right."

Piotr torqued the yoke while Francois sent over the precise heading. They careened straight into an enormous fist of deep brown cloud, and with a final bang against the hull and a flutter, the ship broke through to smooth air.

They'd found the eddy. They were safe, for now.

Francois sank back in his seat and let out an enormous sigh.

Piotr mopped the sweat from his brow with his sleeve—and wanted to curse a blue streak at Francois for taking his sweet old time—but couldn't help smiling with more than a bit of smug self-satisfaction at the mighty fine bit of flying he'd just pulled off. "That was a helluva ride, if I do say so myself."

Piotr released the clasp on his harness and looked over his shoulder.

And his smile vanished right quick.

Amalthea obviously wasn't impressed.

In fact, she hadn't even bothered to put her helmet on for that little bout of turbulence.

She was slouched in her seat, fast asleep.

FIVE

THE PRESSURE MOUNTED.

Five kilobars, ten kilobars, twenty.

But no helium rain, not a trace of the long-theorized hydrogen slush.

Just a murk that got deeper and darker and hotter in an unrelenting gradient of death.

Either the theorists had some recalculating to do, or Piotr was going to have to pilot this ship a lot deeper than he'd bargained for.

Perhaps both.

Viewport synthesis was fully engaged now.

What they saw and heard and even smelled was not so much the actuality of what lay beyond the viewscreen, but Bayesian inferences on the torrents of information collected by the acutely tuned sensor arrays. The viewsynth took it all in and rendered everything comprehensible to the severely limited dynamic range of human perception.

The ship had taken on the strong unmistakable odor of ammonia even though there was very little of it, as far as Piotr could tell, in the gloam beyond the viewscreens. Perhaps it was the viewsynth, perhaps it was a strange perceptual illusion, or perhaps there were unsuspected flaws in the hull after all.

The magnetic fields inside the ship crept higher despite the Herculean labors of the hull's intricate superconducting carapace. Five point two Tesla and rising.

Soon there would be consequences.

Francois and Amalthea had been huddled together at the entrance to the cargo hold for over an hour now. Amalthea sat cross-legged in front of Francois and seemed to enjoy the eye contact a little too much. Every time Piotr glanced back Amalthea seemed to have scuttled ever so slightly forward, leaned in a little bit closer to Francois.

They sure as hell weren't discussing the finer points of the cargo's weight distribution, that was for sure.

Piotr couldn't tell what they were saying, or even what they were talking about. It made him feel distinctly unsettled and he didn't like that about himself or the whole situation.

Not one bit. He was supposed to be the pilot after all, the one in control, and he almost found himself wishing for another bout of severe turbulence, or even some minor breach of the hull so he would have something to do but think about Amalthea and Francois and fume.

So instead he tried to focus on the Great Red. The Enormous Bloody Maelstrom of Jupiter.

The anti-cyclone of his mind.

Beyond the jaundiced wraiths of cloud loomed a dark form, a towering ruddy nimbus that buttressed the sky. Below the ship, ghostly aurorae shimmered in hazes of ultramarine and deep violet, and fluted white veils of fog scintillated with frozen diamonds. Keyholes flashed open to Stygian landscapes of seething gaseous magma only to vanish again before Piotr could behold their glowering majesty.

The truth of Jupiter, always veiled in mists, always shrouded in mysteries deeper and darker still.

The foul smell of the ammonia intensified, the horrid rotten-egg stench of sulfides clambered fist-over-fist up his tongue and shoved their way down his throat. The hull's intricately woven substrates—microscopic Manhattans of semiconductor traces and Casmir voids and meta-materials laced with rare earth metals—cocooned the ship in a quantum miracle that could deflect a billion rads of hardened radiation or dissuade a magnetic field that'd bolt Zeus to the floor. But somehow still the stench outside—or the even worse stench within that clung to their bodies—found a way to ferment and intensify in the steaming meaty stew of their exhalations.

Two men, one woman.

Seven days, no showers.

Ninety-four degrees, ninety-five percent humidity.

And getting thicker and hotter and more intolerable with each passing second. A recipe for contempt and disgust, if not outright hostility.

It was not a pretty picture.

Piotr scanned the instrument read-outs once again. The pressure gauges twitched edgily towards the far side of the orange band, threatening to creep into the red. The quantum counter-pressure fields sandwiched into the hulls were holding, but showing signs of decaying coherence.

One oversight in their calculations or manufacture, one tiny structural flaw, and the hull would implode in a millisecond.

If not faster.

And as their bodies instantly became no more than a smear on the great seething maelstrom of Jupiter, the tempest would blow just a bit ruddier, scream just a bit louder, and then every last trace of their existence—even the dreams and nightmares that we like to believe can transcend any one life and give meaning to humanity, yet which inexorably fall silent with the last breath of the individual who most holds them sacred—

These too would be eradicated from the universe.

Gone.

"I'm not sure how much longer she can hold," Piotr said. "I won't have everyone's blood on my hands." He steepled his fingers, then collapsed a loose fist into his own palm, rubbed his hands in one another over and over again in a futile effort to cleanse them. He hated to say it, but he'd found nothing. He hadn't resolved a thing. Gunther was still dead and the fury of the storm only intensified, circling faster and deeper and darker as it spiraled into itself.

His mood thickened and gathered darkness.

He dropped his forehead into his fists and knuckled the flesh of his scalp taut against his skull, as if he were trying to escape some conclusion imprisoned within.

But he wasn't thinking of himself when he spoke.

"It might be time to turn back."

Amalthea rose to her feet.

"No—don't do it. We can't turn back now. We haven't gone deep enough."

"Deep enough for what? To prove we can smash ourselves, crush our own souls?"

She gave Piotr that don't-tread-on-me look. The one she got when the summit was within reach, or on those couple of occasions when he'd had too much to drink, and tried to get too close.

"All I know," Amalthea said, "is that we can't give up now."

"But why?"

"We have to know. *I* have to know." She ran her fingers through the black loom of her hair. "We can't turn back without seeing how far we can push this—we'll never have this opportunity again. We have to find the metallic hydrogen."

Francois stood and walked up behind her, firmed a protective (possessive?) hand on her shoulder. "Either that, or prove it doesn't exist."

Amalthea twisted her shoulder free of Francois' grip and pressed in close to Piotr, getting right in his face. Lightning zigzagged in the viewsynth and the reflection of the thunderbolts emblazoned her eyes with tiny electrified rivers. "How about you, hotshot? Why are you doing this?"

Piotr's blood steamed now, he thrust himself right up out of his seat and towered over her. "You want to know why? I'll tell you why."

He took a deep breath and gestured vehemently at the thickening crimson murk beyond the viewscreen.

"I want to say the hell with it. I want to throw my life into the profound screaming whoosh of the world's biggest toilet. My brother is dead. I don't want self-realization, I want self-dissolution. I want to go to the brink and beyond. I want to hurl myself into the pit, feel the world reeling in madness round the sinking feeling in my guts. I want to be stabbed by fear, stalked by madness, dizzied by terror. And there is only one place to find that, only one place that can howl with the tempest of my soul."

"I look out the windscreen into this clamorous red vortex, and I see myself and I see my fate and I see my brother's blood, coursing in blind eddies as it screams for oxygen, as he lies suffocating beneath the intense frozen pressure of the avalanche in the darkness and wonders why he can't hear my voice, why he can't hear the sounds of me digging him out."

Amalthea nodded slowly, her eyes welling with tears as she finished the thought for him. "And so you think if you can fathom the Great Red, then somehow you'll find him, somehow you'll claw Gunther free."

Francois crossed his arms in front of his chest, his head shaking. "Gunther's dead and you can't change that. Even if you kill us all, you won't find your answers here."

"All right, Francy-pants, if you're so smart, why did you sign on for this?"

Francois angled his jaw down slightly and bit hard on his bottom lip. He stayed that way a long time without a word. There was something Francois wasn't saying, some doubt mushrooming in his mind.

Piotr glared back at him, Amalthea held alabaster still.

And then Francois spoke.

"You're the one she loves," he said. "But I'm the one who couldn't live if she were dead."

Francois swept a broad gesture at the storm outside. "So you and me, let's get to the bottom of this howling red bitch, find that goddamned metallic hydrogen, and see if she's bloody well worth it."

Francois turned away and scrabbled at his brow as he studied how he might rearrange the cargo yet again. Piotr thought he was done, but then he spoke once more.

"Because I'm not going back without an answer—a crystal clear bloody answer—one way or another."

SIX

THE INCANDESCENT HAZY STRATA SHROUDED boiling convection cells of white-hot quicksilver. Lenticular clouds stacked layer upon layer in spectacular iridescent knife-blades that gleamed like a murderous prism. They radiated not the warmth of the far-off sun but the seething rage of a giant planet, of a failed star, of a world stifled for nearly five billion years by the extreme crushing pressure of its own bulk.

The sensors chirped and shrieked at the presence, at long last, of the metallic hydrogen, of the substance which had erected itself in Piotr's febrile mind into a near-mythical Colossus of adamantine and platinum.

Despite the nano-scale Manhattan cocooning the hull, the field lines spun up by the intense metallic hydrogen dynamo of Jupiter pulsed through the cabin with nearly ten Tesla of magnetic flux. Piotr's mind reeled somewhere in a liminal zone between dizziness and arousal. His solar plexus churned and he felt like he might pass out. His mind was giddy with confabulation, paralyzed by impending terror.

Piotr's heart raced.

His temples pounded with a pressure far beyond the worst that Jupiter could hurl at him.

But he knew that had to ask her, or he could never turn back, never face himself again.

"Is it true what Francois said—" he held her gaze, refused to look away. "Amalthea, do you love me?"

She crossed her arms stiffly in front of her chest, her cold blue eyes wide and deep and welling with tears like a moulin waiting to collapse into the deep ultramarine midnight of a glacier.

"I was in love once," Amalthea said, but then the mesmeric gaze of Jupiter beguiled her once more.

Her eyes lost their focus and seemed to dance with the writhing bands of superfluidic steam. Piotr imagined she sought some wisp of certainty, some anchor in the ever-shifting monuments of vapor and convection columns that welled up from the underworlds of Jupiter, rising like the phantom tombstones of a towering spectral cemetery. It was a vista of death so incomprehensibly expansive that not even the restive souls of all the world's dead—the untold billions who had lived, lost, and mourned—could possibly hope to account for it.

The vision rivaled Piotr's inner landscape, brought it into a brilliant poignant focus that summoned tears to his eyes. Only the intense expectancy of the moment— the surface tension of his hot-salt tears, the electricity that crackled in the air, the incomprehensible pressure which bore down on his mind from every conceivable direction— held him together. He was like one of those strange spiny creatures discovered huddled around a deep-sea vent, phosphorescing and unknown to science, that would burst into a confusion of briny protoplasm if he were brought to the surface.

"He was killed in a motorcycle accident—" Amalthea began.

Her breath hitched and Piotr saw that her eyes, too, were about to overflow with tears.

He instinctively took a half-step forward, but she fended him off with an open palm, held a knuckle to her lip.

She gasped, choked down some deep hurt that had long yearned to escape her—and went on.

"—three months before the wedding."

Tears let loose, streamed down her face now, seemed to steam into the hot dense atmosphere of the ship as she spoke, even to plume out of the hull and diffuse into the immense bulwarks of Jupiter's skulking gloom.

Amalthea inhaled sharply and continued. "Afterwards I threw myself into the High Sierra. Took solace in the spired cathedrals. Prostrated my soul before the blinding white fields of sun-cupped snow. It was an escape—a savage, black-pinnacled salvation."

Piotr nodded his head in understanding. "And then I came along," he said.

"No, you vain, self-absorbed fool. I met Francois. And I thought I could love again."

"I thought—" Piotr started, confusion furrowing his brow.

Amalthea cut him off. "But I was wrong."

"About Francois? He's a fine and clever gentleman, if you believe in alphabetizing your socks." Piotr's feint at humor wrung a smile from Amalthea's lips, but the tears did not stop flowing down her cheeks.

"No. I was wrong about love. It's the intricate crystal chalice of our souls—once it's crushed, it's shattered forever."

"So you came to the Great Red Spot of Jupiter."

"You pulled me in."

"You wouldn't take no for an answer."

"You're mistaking me for Francois," Amalthea replied.

"That's hardly possible. His man-boobs are big and hairy, for one thing."

"Ha ha. You still think you're funny, don't you?"

"If you think getting quashed by a hundred thousand bars of pressure under dense ugly brown clouds that reek like a lounge full of smokers who haven't brushed their teeth in a month, for nothing more than a scant hope of sucking up a test-tube full of an overblown metallic turd—well if you think that's funny, then yeah, I'm a laugh riot."

Amalthea wasn't laughing. Not even smiling. She crossed her arms again. "So what are you going to do about Gunther?"

Piotr's lips drew taut across his teeth. He tongued the saliva off his gums, felt the sharp ridges of his canines bite into the tip of his tongue. "Maybe—with enough heat, with enough pressure—maybe it's possible to anneal even yourself. To build a pyre beneath the memories of the dead. To summon a conflagration so fierce and so hot and so unrelenting that there is no choice but to forge your soul anew."

Amalthea leaned in, tilted up her jaw, thrust forward.

And kissed him.

He wrapped his arms tight around her, felt the press of her breasts against his chest even through the stiff, thick layers of his suit—and hers. He allowed himself to wonder for the first time how she would feel, the delicious warm pressure of her bare skin, without it.

Then Piotr kissed her harder.

He wasn't quite sure if the sensations—the warm tingling wave that washed through his body, the cool flux of relief that pulsated through the dark folded crevices his mind, the visage of his brother that suddenly seemed to rear itself in a fog bank and then just as abruptly dissolve back into formlessness—were real, or if the intense magnetic fields were seriously messing with his head.

Either way, for the first time in a really, really long time he liked what he saw before him, and he liked even more how it made him feel inside.

Piotr shuddered with pleasure at the sense of looming triumph that was starting to come over him, and he decided right then he was going to see this thing through to the end.

SEVEN

THE SHIP LURCHED as the ruddy murk dissipated, and the relentless fury of Jupiter's liquid-metallic dynamo revealed itself at last.

Great fountains of quicksilver lashed themselves together in tremendous arches, coiled and twined, sparked with bristling needles and giga-ampere electrical discharges. They stood like the platinum-plated skeletons of colossal fleshless beasts, spines whipsawing and braying, exposed nerves branching out in savage barbs of gleaming liquid metal.

The forms reminded Piotr of the ferro-fluidic sculptures of a deranged artist he'd once seen, whirling horned monstrosities that spun and clawed at the air with impossible quivering talons.

Only this was an exalted landscape nearly beyond human conception, the entire core of the largest planet in the solar system, and its furor knew no worldly bounds.

The field lines snapped and exploded. Vast bolts continuously discharged. Pincushions of metallic hydrogen burst in front of Piotr's eyes like silvered shards of an exploding god.

Deeper down, the field lines were stable enough that the mercurial hydrogen clung to them in quicksilver buttresses of a heraldic Jovian cathedral. Between the gleaming arches monstrous black voids, caverns and meanders and sinkholes beckoning to oblivion, gaped within the ocean of liquid-metallic hydrogen.

Piotr tilted the yoke forward, full bore, and they plunged into their final descent.

The hull pinged and cracked ceaselessly as if the oil sealed in an industrial cauldron had reached its critical temperature. The three-man shuddered and dropped. Piotr's teeth clamped together and he tasted blood in his mouth. His head slammed into the headrest and pitched forward till his helmet bounced off his chest and then jostled side to side. He was no longer certain of what was him, what sensations were actually inside his own body and mind, or just contrivances synthesized by the sensor array for his benefit—or perhaps, even, an electromagnetic halo of religious awe evoked by the long-veiled deity lurking within the core of Jupiter itself.

For a moment Piotr saw himself from afar, detached from his circumstance, and he watched the broken machine of his body as it struggled to cope with this new reality. He saw the field-lines interacting with the iron in the hemoglobin of his blood, he saw the enormous electromagnetic forces distorting his thoughts and perceptions and desires, bending them to the will of Jupiter, conjuring visions that no human had ever beheld before.

Quicksilver serpents coiled round the ship. Forked metallic tongues scented the hull, seemed to lick at the folds of his mind. He saw their silver-plated jaws unhinge as they tried to swallow down his memories of Gunther in one bulging gulp, he felt the coils of their bodies, the texture of their gleaming scalloped scales, tightening round and round his nascent love for Amalthea.

He had to decide.

Piotr flicked the stainless steel toggle switch, the one control he had not yet touched on the entire descent into the Great Red Spot of Jupiter, and parted the containment fields briefly to let the Casmir-containment trap fill with a tiny sample of the metallic hydrogen. The viewsynth showed a rendering of it quivering and coming to rest, a perfect spherical bubble that glinted with the inner majesty of Jupiter like an embryo of salvation.

He pulled back on the yoke and the ship started to rise. Immense shimmering arches of metallic hydrogen rushed past outside.

Piotr flicked his private view over to an oblique vantage of Amalthea, saw the sparkle in her eyes as she gazed in wonderment at the vista materializing before them.

Piotr smiled. At that moment he could not recall the bite of melting snow crystals on his skin or what it felt like to be trapped cold and suffocating under the hardening snow or even the face of his own brother at that eternally frozen moment he had last seen him alive.

He knew he had not forgotten, but at the same time he could not remember. Not in specifics, not in detail, not with the vividness of grief.

He looked at Amalthea and sensed the possibility there and knew he had, at long last, begun to heal.

In the sprawling mists and intense forges of Jupiter, the crystalline memory of grief had finally eased, like a glacier that had slid loose of its long-frozen deep moorings.

Piotr beheld the gleaming silver cathedrals at the heart of Jove and remembered Gunther as he remembered him best in life, in the midst of an epic climb. One knee locked with his boot firmly planted in hard-packed snow. The other foot swinging free, kicking forcefully at the unyielding snow, always reaching one step higher.

Piotr's mind rose giddily with the ship, soaring up and out as it strove for the incredible two hundred and fifteen thousand kilometer-per-hour escape velocity of Jupiter, enraptured with the prospect of a long and luminous lifetime in Amalthea's soft embrace.

A final squall buffeted the ship as he wrestled with the controls, seemed to whisper in Piotr's ear with Gunther's spectral voice.

Was it the viewsynth? Was it ten Tesla of magnetic flux?

Perhaps, but Piotr chose to believe something else.

"When the sun breaks, touch the top for me," Gunther's voice seemed to whisper with the wind, echo from the cathedral vaults at the sacred heart of Jupiter—

"And don't ever look back."

4

FEATHERS OF FROST, FEATHERS OF FLAME

ON THE SEVENTH NIGHT OF HIS VIGIL the kiln incandesced with white-hot grief, sublimated tears from the molten-glass embers of Kaleetan's eyes. He repeated the words to himself for the thousandth time, still unable to believe: *Viridian is dead.* He raked his forehead with callused fingers, tried to till the frozen wound from his mind, but it was a futile gesture. *My bride, my love, my purpose lies dead.*

Grimcliffe approached from the broad fieldstone archway of the crematorium, arms extended, a linen-wrapped parcel bridging his palms.

"The hour of the prophecy looms."

Grimcliffe's beetling white brows peaked above wizened eyes. An unpigmented polyp, a permanent teardrop of flesh, glimmered from his tear duct like a distant snowfield in the dim light. "It is time to anneal the blade."

Kaleetan did not look Grimcliffe straight in the eye, gave him no nod of acknowledgement. What could the elders know of his suffering? Just one week ago he had stood hand in hand with his bride, their future rising before them like an unmarred panorama of alpine glory, and then—

Kaleetan stared past Grimcliffe, through the stone archway, at the snowcapped peaks beyond.

The Sentinel of Fury, the highest mountain in all of Cascadia, dominated the moonlit vista. Avalanche chutes gripped its savage flanks as if the snows were the skeletal fingers of frozen gods risen up to reclaim this profane black spire of the earth. Lenticular clouds stacked layer by layer in the lee of the summit, halberds of the sky assaulting the exalted dominion of hoarfrost and glaciers above the timberline.

It was an aerie far above the concerns of men—a realm of dragons and curses, prophecies and sacrifice, and from it the White Death tormented all the land.

But if the prophecy were true…

Kaleetan took the parcel from Grimcliffe's hands and unwound the grubby white linen. The leather-wrapped hilt of the sword stank of man-sweat and fear. The lusterless silver blade bloomed with lichens of heavy tarnish. *How could this be it,* he thought, *the Sword of the Silver Mists?*

He wanted no part of this struggle.

How can I give up Viridian, all of eternity in The Verdant Country with my love, for this tarnished blade of false gods and fallen kings?

And yet here he stood. The bearer of the prophecy, the man who had lost everything. The man who could still, perhaps, free Cascadia from the clutches of the White Death.

If he could ascend to the summit.

If he had the courage to make the right choice, sacrifice his love, and summon the feathers of flame.

If he lived to plunge the blade through the dark cyclonic heart of the beast, to slay the White Death.

It was as Grimcliffe said: without hope, the age of frost would hold dominion over Cascadia without end.

He had to try, didn't he? Winter had gripped Cascadia for seven years. How long could they subsist on frozen roots and dried venison? Damn the elders. He owed Viridian that much, he owed his brothers that much, he owed the people of Cascadia that much.

No matter how terrible the price.

For he had already lost Viridian in death.

And if he were victorious, he would lose her once more. For all of eternity. No Verdant Country, no life everlasting.

Tonight was the first step of the journey.

Kaleetan squeezed the hilt in his fist, saw the cords of muscle erupt and quiver within his flesh, and then he thrust it as far into the heart of the kiln as he could bear. The air filled with the tang of singed hair and the sizzle of boiling sweat. He watched the sword until the leather smoked and burst into flame, until the pommel glowed bright red.

He took the solid iron rake from the wall of the crematory and reached into the kiln. He banked gray dust and shards of bone against the left side of the blade, against the right. He spread the ashes of his bride up and down the tarnished silver shaft, left only the hilt protruding.

And then he sat back against the stone wall of the crematory, arms crossed over his torso, and waited for dawn of the eighth day—his final dawn—to break.

* * *

KALEETAN DREAMED of the Verdant Country. The sawgrass was a lush cadmium green, the sun a luminous gold, the breeze heavy with the scent of subalpine harebells and phlox. Even the stones scattered across the alpine meadow radiated warmth, encrustations of lichens aflame with muted reds and yellows.

Viridian's fingers filled the void of his palm. He worked his thumb greedily across the back of her hand, plying her satin skin, lingering in the valleys between her knuckles. Her flesh coursed with life.

He knew he should not do it, that it would break the spell, but he could bear her absence no longer. He turned to behold her breathtaking face once more, to peer into the glacier-blue of her eyes, her pupils gaping black moulins pouring vast sorrows into her soul…

They stood in the chapel again; he heard the sound first. . A rumbling slowly crested, shaking the candlelit glass globes of the chandelier, vibrating the stained glass in the tall, narrow stone windows. A harbinger of the White Death thundered down the mountain, stampeding towards the village, smashing all that stood in its path to flinders.

And then the avalanche burst into the structure, cleaved the chapel in two, tore his bride from his outstretched palms.

Afterwards fragments of stone archways and splintered hemlock buttresses protruded from the snow. He dug and dug with his bare hands until they were numb, until they went blue, until they bled scarlet on unyielding snow.

But of Viridian's understated smile, her sublime gaze, he saw no more.

* * *

WHEN KALEETAN AWOKE the fire was out, the ashes were cold.

The seventh night had passed.

His lungs plumed false dragon's breath. Through the vacant stone archway cold light illuminated clouds rafted together like enormous gray skulls, a foreboding ossuary of the skies that leered down at him.

But when Kaleetan stood, the sterling pommel of the Sword of the Silver Mists shimmered from the heart of the kiln.

Kaleetan raked the ashes and fragments of bleached-white bone away from the blade, drew them to the opening. Could this really be all that was left of her, of his beloved Viridian? He dreaded recognizing some contour, the cusp of a tooth, perhaps the hollow of a knuckle or the exquisite curve of her chin. He shuddered and brushed her remains into a modest leather pouch, careful to gather every last grain of dust.

He turned his attention to the sword. He grasped the hilt in his fist, pulled it from the kiln. Without the leather it was cold and smooth, its grip the perfect reverse of his fingers. The blade still did not shimmer. The tarnish was gone but it was now encrusted with fine gray powder, the edge of the blade serrated with shards of white bone.

The dust of her flesh, the splinters of her soul.

Kaleetan had annealed the blade—at midnight on the seventh day, just as the prophecy demanded—with the ashes of his virgin bride.

Viridian had made a great sacrifice, though she had never chosen it in life.

And now it was time for Kaleetan to do the same.

But before he departed, he stared one last time into the cold empty kiln. He needed something to take with him. Some small totem of his vigil, of his trial by fire and ice.

He worked at the mouth of the kiln, back and forth, pushing and prying, until a single granite cobble—two fists wide, one fist deep—came loose in his cracked and bleeding palms.

With it he would lay the first course of her tomb.

* * *

KALEETAN TUGGED THE LEATHER STRAPS of his rucksack tight one last time and stepped onto the snowfield.

Cascadia would not blossom with spring again until Kaleetan stood on the summit and plunged his blade through the dark cyclonic heart of the beast. So said the elders, so said Grimcliffe, so said the prophecy.

But if he failed, the White Death would lord over the world for a thousand years.

And so Kaleetan climbed.

He kicked the wide mesh of his snowshoe into the slope, locked his knee, and levered himself one step higher. Kick, step, kick. Kick, step, kick. Over and over again, until the movement itself crystallized, like a scalloped cornice of hard-packed snow, another repeating pattern locked forever in frost.

* * *

GRIMCLIFFE STOOD IN THE ARCHWAY of the crematory and watched the tiny black speck rise ever so slowly up the shoulder of the Sentinel of Fury.

He was a brave boy, Kaleetan, but hopefully not brave enough to do anything foolish. Just brave enough to do what Grimcliffe had asked of him, just brave enough to fulfill the prophecy—and no more.

One had to hope. Without hope, there was nothing. Without hope, the age of ice and snow—The White Death—would rule Cascadia without end…

* * *

WHEN HE KNEW WHICH WAY TO GO he picked a couloir, another forked tongue of snow, and climbed higher. He wedged his wool-gloved hands into cracks, thrust his body up narrow black chimneys of stone, and emerged onto snowfields higher still.

He tried not to dwell on the steepening slope that disappeared between his legs. When he ascended into cloud he was almost glad of it; if he could not see the way forward, neither could he see the beckoning abyss below. In the cloud the air grew colder, the wind kicked up, and tiny daggers of wind-whipped snow lashed at his face. When the slope abated cracks appeared in the snow, bottomless chasms filled only by an unearthly shade of deep gloaming blue.

These he stepped over, and swallowed hard, but kept climbing.

At long last Kaleetan crested the ridgeline, festooned with windswept cornices and sinister black pinnacles of ice-mantled rock. Gales howled and whooped, a blasphemous psalm of false gods. The storm, the White Death, gathered its fury.

He couldn't be far from the top now, and the Frost Dragon would be waiting.

The wind blew right through his overcoats, drained what little warmth remained in his soul. Icy fingers crept up his hand, the gelid embrace of a dying lover. He remembered Viridian when they had finally dug her out of the avalanche debris, her impossibly cold hand hanging limp in his own, the flaccid chill of death on her lips when he kissed her for the last time.

Kaleetan crested a final rise and stood at the summit of Fury. The wind had sculpted the ice-blocks of the summit snowfield into a strange congregation of shapes, misshapen deep-shadowed maws and hunched-over penitents that bowed before the gale. The tempest whirled and thrashed, tongues of frost licked at his face, great shushing feathers of it lashed at his skin.

The mists cleared for a moment and he had a glimpse of the beast.

The scale of it stunned him. Its body stretched to the horizon, its frost-feathered wings of cirrus rose a thousand fathoms or more into the chill wastes of the firmament. The great nimbus of its head turned on him, its cyclopean eye a leering black vortex swirling in white cloud. The Frost Dragon dwarfed any one mountain. Even the Sentinel of Fury was but a single black fang, one insignificant canine in its monstrous gaping white maw.

Kaleetan unsheathed the blade, the Sword of the Silver Mists, and plunged it like a wayward silver cross into the snow.

He did not need it yet.

Instead he pulled out the leather sack, loosened the drawstring, and prayed to whatever gods might still hold sway here to lend him courage, to help him face his choice with wisdom.

Viridian was dead. There was nothing he could do to bring her back. He had to find the courage to let her go, now and forever. Not just to live without her, but to lose her for all of eternity.

To save Cascadia, he had to offer her ashes to the wind, to let his own chance at salvation slip through his fingers. When he died, his own ashes would not be mingled with hers. They would not be forever entombed together.

For Kaleetan and Viridian there would be no afterlife, no love everlasting.

He had to forsake the vision of The Verdant Country.

Tears streamed down his face, boiled off in frost smoke with the wind. His hands shook. His teeth ground, his jaw ached. Kaleetan closed his eyes, imagined one final glimpse of the Verdant Country, and then pulled off his woolen gloves.

The wind clawed at his skin but he pain it no heed. He turned the leather sack upside-down, let the ashes and shards of bone avalanche into the frozen chalice of his palm.

He extended his fingers, arm outstretched, and offered Viridian to the wind. The gusts took up her ashes in tiny whirlwinds, buffeted the shattered fragments of bone until they too rolled from his palm and fell into the snow.

He tipped the sack higher, let all of her remains spill through his splayed fingers.

The ashes spiraled higher and higher, began to incandesce with a deep seething orange. The filaments of fire assembled themselves layer by layer into burning fronds of feathers, into the great flaming plumage of wings. The ashes were gone but still a vortex of flame exploded from his palm, loomed higher and larger and more formidable in the sky.

It was Viridian reborn, a firebird atop the Summit of Fury, a phoenix of vengeance and lost love that reared up in the sky and entwined the spiral arms of her wings around the hundred-mile body of the Frost Dragon.

Colossal streamers of fire and ice braided themselves together as the tempest twisted and whirled. The skies hissed, the entire atmosphere of the Earth crackled and spat and shook. Black thunderheads burst from the swirling interstices of fire and ice, crackled with lightning, boomed with monstrous claps of thunder.

Kaleetan caught glimpses of cloud capped by bloodied white claws, black-singed feathers rimed with frost, winged sheets of flame that girded the horizon. The summit snowfield of Fury shook with the blows, the entire mountain shuddered with their struggle. Cracks rent the snowfield, fresh crevasses yawned wide with a vision of deep-frozen hell. Cornices avalanched onto the slopes below. Tottering pillars of rock had stood sentinel over the summit for millennia collapsed and stood before the wind no more.

Across the summit, a black-cloaked figure rose from the mists.

He moved deliberately, a gnarled wooden alpenstock in hand, picking his way carefully over the crevasses and fallen rock, until he stood with Kaleetan at the summit of Fury.

The man drew back his cowl. His long white hair streamed in the gale, the frozen tear stood pale and motionless at the corner of his eye.

Grimcliffe shouted into the wind.

"With you the prophecy will vanish, hope will die. The power of the White Death will be mine, and mine alone. I will lord over Cascadia unhindered, a thousand year reign of frost without end."

Grimcliffe threw back his arms, held his alpenstock to the sky. A halo of deep violet blazed around his body and then filaments of lightning zigzagged through the storm, bathed Grimcliffe and the broken summit-blocks in an eerie blue-white glow of sublime frozen terror. Thunderclaps exploded, lightning stroked through his body again and again, but Grimcliffe did not flinch, the man did not fall. He stood and gathered the power of the storm, thrust his arms against the sky, and then he was swept up onto the wind, onto the frozen streamers of cloud.

Grimcliffe rode upon the White Death.

Kaleetan seized the Sword of the Silver Mists. He parried cloudbursts of enormous frozen hailstones, flashes of lightning, spindrift that stung his eyes with tiny blinding shards of ice hurled by the wind.

He heard a deep-throated whooping growl far above, gathering speed and force, until finally a savage blast of hoarfrost knocked him backwards onto the snow, scoured him with pellets of ice, left him a carcass of flash-frozen meat barely able to rise from the snow.

And tore the Sword of the Silver Mists from his fingers.

The blade spun away on the wind. The whorls of fire in the sky flickered and died under the relentless onslaught of the gusts of white frost. The phoenix, its feathers of flame summoned with the ashes of Kaleetan's virgin bride, was losing the battle.

Grimcliffe had turned on him. The prophecy of the ancient ones had failed Kaleetan in his hour of need. It had all been for nothing. Kaleetan's sacrifice had been an empty gesture. Now he would die; Viridian was lost; and with the loss of her ashes their chance for love everlasting in the Verdant Country had evaporated on the wind.

The gale gathered with renewed force. Kaleetan glimpsed Grimcliffe one last time, riding the frozen nimbus of the Frost Dragon's head. Now Grimcliffe wielded the Sword of the Silver Mists, gleaming with hoarfrost, the tip aimed right at Kaleetan's chest.

Kaleetan had time to think of only one thing, one small remembrance that might redeem him, and then the frigid point of the blade and an avalanche of frozen wrath was upon him, crushing him into the snow.

The blade ran through Kaleetan and his chest exploded in an intricate lattice of ice crystals. The frost arrested his breath in his lungs, encrusted his skin with delicate finials of frost. The blade gleamed with a dense rime of hoarfrost, Grimcliffe's pale fist clenched about its hilt, even as Kaleetan lashed out with the cobble of granite, a single stone two fists wide and one fist deep.

The cobble struck the blade where it met the hilt, shattered the silver blade into a jagged fang that mirrored the savage Fury of the Sentinel itself.

Grimcliffe's momentum flung him forward, impaled him—the master of the Frost Dragon, the master of the White Death—on the shattered blade.

Kaleetan's blood washed over the gray ash and shards of Viridian's bone encrusting the blade, the final embrace of the doomed lovers. The hoarfrost flashed to steam, the blade scintillated with the white-hot incandescence of the kiln. The jagged end pierced Grimcliffe's heart, black blood ran from the slit in his chest, the frozen white tear in the corner of his eye melted and dropped away—

A final monstrous white flash of lightning exploded, thundered with a single ice-rending clap, and the Frost Dragon shredded on the gale, so many writhing wisps of silent mist carried away on the wind.

The storm abated, breaks in the cloud appeared. Sunbursts of brilliant yellow light shone through.

The White Death reigned upon the crest of Cascadia no more.

* * *

IN TIME THE ICE-CAP MELTED ALTOGETHER, and the men and women of Cascadia made their midsummer pilgrimages to the cadmium-green grasses that girded the summit of the Sentinel of Fury. They paid homage to the granite cobble— one fist deep, two fists wide—lodged in the roots of a subalpine fir that had taken hold there, boughs repentant before the wind, needles silver-green and tipped with fresh growth in sublime sprays of viridian.

They gathered stones, shards of white granite, great angular fangs of black slate, and piled them course by course upon the cobble, the first stone to be laid in the cairn at the apex of the Verdant Country.

5

THE SENSEI OF DANDELIONS HUSHED

A Great Serendipity Scott Adventure in the White Sands of the Trinity Atomic Test Site

THE FOOTFALLS OF MY BOOTS CRUSHED into the perfection of the stark white dunes, the gypsum sand compacting with a distinctive high-pitched crunching sound that could have been the cut-off shrieks of dying souls.

Black anvil clouds massed on the horizon, the dry, hot wind stung my eyes with the infinitesimal white grains whipped up by the gathering storm front.

But I had to push forward into the desert, the *Jornada del Muerto*, I had to mar the sublime grace of the White Sands. The Trinity Test Site, July 15th, 1945, about five o'clock in the evening. It was the last day of innocence, a time and a place like no other on Earth.

Soon the sun would set.

For if I did not find the inimitable Mr. Scott and his consort before the following dawn, we would all be vaporized afore the sun graced God's wretched Earth again.

* * *

A FIELD OF DANDELIONS EXPLODING with brilliant yellow florets, the shards of fallen suns.

I'd pulled on my black mountaineering boots, just as Scott had requested of me, for whatever reason—"Weer yer boots, ya bloody fairy," I could still hear him barking into the phone that morning, in a rare moment when his boyhood accent had taken a hold of him. It had mostly faded from his speech-patterns now, but sometimes he had a strange way of talking, a mangled English accent colored by his time in Mumbai, his mixed heritage, and his brief residences in a long succession of second-rate American cities. That is, until he settled into his stately craftsman upon the top of

Queen Anne Hill in Seattle and brought me into his employ, of course.

I looked down at those tight-laced black boots of mine and suddenly found myself afraid I would trample the glorious blossoms of the dandelions beneath my tread.

Yes, they were weeds, and they really were that beautiful.

The park squatted just beyond the asphalt grasp of a strip mall. An old lady shuffled into a doctor's office while her husband held the door for her, a mother pushed a twin stroller up the sidewalk to a scented candle boutique. The park wasn't much of a park, one of those cubby-hole parks the urban planners like to squeeze into the sprawling 'burbs to get over their guilt at having bulldozed the meadows that came before. This one had nothing but a couple of spar-varnished fir benches and the dandelions, not even a play-structure for over-exuberant children. But for some reason beyond my comprehension, Mr. Scott's client, one Shizuko Katani, had insisted we meet her there.

So there we sat, Mr. Scott and I, waiting to see what the wind would blow in.

Bumblebees buzzed through the close-cropped grass, visiting the dandelions one by one. The assault of pollen brought a puffiness to my cheeks. I pulled out my iPhone—it was 1:26, the woman now nearly a half-hour late. I was ready to kiss off, but Mr. Scott seemed unconcerned, perhaps a reflection of his adamant refusal to bill by the hour. All I knew was that she had once been a high priestess of a little-known branch of the Japanese Shinto faith, a woman under whom Mr. Scott had studied many years ago, and had great respect for. He scrawled in his little black book whatever biddings his subconscious whispered to him with his Mont Blanc fountain pen, which he dipped periodically into the Mystery Black ink bottoming the inkwell that he always carried on his person.

Yes, they actually call it that, Mystery Black, and I can assure you that he is rather attached to that particular shade.

I've long since stopped questioning his methods. Results are results, however they come about, and I think by now his track record speaks for itself.

A black Mercedes E-class sedan pulled into the handicapped stall, the parking spot closest to where we sat, and crept forward hesitantly until the tires jumped half way up the curb and settled back. The windows, deep tinted, sparkled in the sun. The door swung open and a frail woman wearing a white pantsuit with black piping, and a white sun-hat ringed with a wide black ribbon, rose from the driver's seat and pulled herself up by the door-handle.

The top of her head barely rose above the roof of the sedan, and even then only because of the scant inches added by the sun hat.

The heavily wrinkled flesh of her face clung close to the skull beneath. There was no stoop to her posture, she stood tall and proud. A tiny white clamshell purse with a gold clasp swung from the peak of her shoulder by a wire-thin white leather strap. She walked to us in short staccato steps, slowly, her white leather shoes scuffing off the concrete sidewalk and into the hush of the dandelions and thick green grass.

Mr. Scott stood, and I took his cue as well. He yanked his business card from his inside breast pocket, a little more clumsily than usual, and a few pinches of snuff that had spilled out of his tin came along for the ride. It was the menthol-flavored Wilson's White Snuff, tobacco free, that he had taken up of late to try and kick the habit, and it plumed over the dandelion-spangled lawn.

He held out the card to her with both hands and bowed with a well-practiced ease.

"Shizuko-sensei, welcome, it is a great honor." The ritual and grace of it told me there was a subtlety to the motion that was specific to this moment, this context with this woman, that I was unable to fully grasp.

I tried to bow anyway, but the brief flash of a scowl on her face told me I'd probably only succeeded in making a fool of myself.

Just one of the many reasons the great Mr. Scott keeps me in his employ. I've found it pays to be useful, and useless, in just about equal measure. Serendipity, a strong dash of his salted with a tiny pinch of my own, fills in the gaps.

Shizuko mirrored Mr. Scott's bow and held the card with both hands, carefully studying the hodgepodge of baroque fonts on the eggshell-white cardstock that he favored.

Since I'd ordered them printed up myself, I knew exactly what it said:

Great Serendipity Scott's
Clearing House of Occult Detecting
and Sundry Peculiarities
Sarin Chandrasankar Scott,
Chief Proprietor

And that was it. Nothing else.

On one occasion I'd deigned to ask him why there wasn't an address, or even so much as a phone number. Wouldn't it be better for business? "Ahhh," he'd said, followed by the sharp inhalation through his nostrils that he was overly fond of affecting. "Folks wit' proper motivation will find me. The rest can take their money straight t'Hell, where it belongs."

After that, I didn't ask any more.

"This is my associate," he said, summoning the most formal voice he could muster, and his bollixed-up accent very nearly disappeared. "Mr. Morrow Walker. He speaks to me, and me only. By which I mean he owes allegiance to no other man."

She worked the gold clasp of her purse with fingers spidered by deep violet veins, knuckles swollen with arthritis, and slipped Mr. Scott's card in there with whatever other diminutive mysteries were huddled within. She closed her eyes briefly as she started to speak.

"Thank you for your attentions, Mees-ter Scott." The way she pronounced his name rhymed with *goat*, and it took me a moment to grasp what she'd said. "I wait long time for these chance. To a-hold her again."

"And you shall. Your English—remarkable, you've come so far in just six months. Your professor has taught you well."

Then he yabbered something at her in Japanese, a tongue utterly alien to me in its ooooh and aaahs and ichi-sans. But I gathered he was asking her how we could help her, what came next.

"Rukoko," she said, as she lowered her eyes and knotted her arthritic fingers together. "My sister. We twin babies. Mother take me to doctor, Father take Rukoko-chan to park—tree garden?—to see maple, cherry, all the flower. "

"You mean to say arboretum? A Japanese garden?"

"Alboretum," she said, trying but not quite managing that 'r' sound. "Yes, that, I mean to say. Tree-garden in city. Beautiful garden with beautiful gazebo, mother tell me. In Nagasaki."

Mr. Scott and I exchanged glances, bowed in our posture ever so slightly. Even now, the brilliant flash of the second atomic bomb ever wielded in anger cast a deep dark shadow upon our peoples, upon history, upon all of humanity. It was a wrong that crowned a long, long line of cruelties that stretched back to antiquity.

"Mother say Father and Rukoko-chan never come back. She wait one year, two year, ten year. No Father. No Rukoko-chan. After she die, my mother, long time pass, I come to America. Move to Seattle. Many beautiful mountain, tall green tree all over. Live here rest of my life. Never go back."

Shizuko Katani had been there in Nagasaki. One of the survivors. Far enough from the blast that she lived to lead a full and prosperous the life.

Her father and sister had been extinguished by the blast.

"Sensei," Mr. Scott said, "I mourn for your loss, I feel the weight of the past on my shoulders." He reached out and cupped her hand in his enormous palms, looked her right in the eyes.

"She my twin," Mrs. Katani said. "I live full life—she live, nothing. Soon—no more. I die."

Tears welled in her eyes, and I could feel tears tugging at my own as well.

"I want—all I want—is hold her, soothe her, love her cheek one time before I dead too."

Mr. Scott nodded, a serious look pressing upon his brow, but said nothing. He kneeled down in the grass upon one knee, bent down low and plucked a single dandelion from the grass, then held it up high as if it might yet rejoin the bright afternoon sun.

"Sensei, if you please, follow me. You shall be well taken care of."

"Thank you, Sarin-san," said, "so it be. I give you my a-trust, my honor."

"Then we must make haste. The sands of time wait for no one." And with that he bowed and started to walk slowly across the rich green grass.

I moved to follow but he waved me off. "Not this time, dear Morrow. I need you here. Wait one hour, and if we don't return, then wait one hour more, and if need be yet another hour after that." He took Mrs. Katani's hand in one palm, cupped her delicate shoulder with the other, and helped her across the park.

He turned to me one last time, spoke in a cold clear diction that sounded so discordant in the flawless golden sunlight. "I will see you again in the white sands, or I won't see you at all."

And with that they shuffled off and around the corner.

I was left to wait, and to wonder, just what in the hell he was talking about.

* * *

You have to understand Mr. Scott. Half of what he spouts is irrational nonsense, but it always works out. Always.

It never makes for an easy journey though, and that's where I come in. Sometimes there are (ahem) problems to be papered over. Gaps to be filled. Things that need fixing in the night.

And sometimes it's just having the patience to remain idle in the brilliance of the afternoon sun.

I waited one hour. I waited two. More old people, and more women with babies in more strollers, came and went from the doctor's office. Somehow the scented candle shop was still in business, despite only three customers cracking open its doors the whole afternoon. The fir slats of the bench pressed a Venetian blind pattern into my derriere as I waited and waited. The sun rounded the sky and threatened to scuttle itself behind the strip mall. I was growing hungry if not desperate. I began to wonder if now might not be the right moment to find another line of work.

The occult is a slow business in this modern world.

Tired of standing, tired of pressing my arse into the bench, I plopped down on the lawn. Tugged the blades of grass with my fingers, watched a bumblebee dance across the dandelions. They seemed to burn orange in the descending arc of the late-afternoon sun.

The dandelions.

I rose to my knees and knelt there. Not in prayer, but perhaps I should have.

I stooped and picked a dandelion, the largest I could find. It seemed preposterous but I didn't know what else to do. I shrugged. Serendipity. You have to trust 'im sometimes.

I held the dandelion out before me and followed the path that Mr. Scott and Mrs. Katani had taken. Followed in their footsteps.

When I turned the corner, no revelation thundered upon me from the heavens. There was more asphalt, some split-rail fencing, some tulips blooming along a row of leaden-gray townhouses all the same.

Of Mrs. Katani and Mr. Scott there was no sign.

I held the dandelion to my nose, closed my puffy eyelids, and inhaled its scent deeply.

With a thunderous dandy of a sneeze stars danced before my eyes and when I opened them again sheets of white sand stung my corneas, peppered my face with a tingling sensation that seemed to be a phantom mask of myself.

With a few steps and the whiff of a single dandelion I had fallen out of space, fallen out of time.

And into the white sands of the *Jornada del Muerto*, the one day's journey of the dead man.

An aptly named place if there ever was one, and it was hotter than a kettle a-boil in Hell, even though the sun was encroaching on the low dunes to the west.

I had no idea where I was, which direction to go.

There were no footprints other than my own, no hint that Mr. Scott or any other living soul had ever been here. The wind-whipped sands drew veils over themselves; even if a man had once shuffled through here, his passage would have soon been lost to the relentless march of time.

I moved toward a tussock of vegetation in the lee of a dune to try and shelter myself from the wind. A clump of silvery-gray grasses were crowned with a soap-tree yucca blossoming in full glory, its creamy-white blossoms glowing in the sun.

I looked closer at its fan of leathery-green fronds and saw something square-cornered peeking out, something utterly out of place, and tugged it out from between the fronds.

It was Mr. Scott's business card. It had been stashed deep within the fronds, hidden away from the wind.

But there had been no doubt in his mind that I would find it. Of that I was certain.

I glanced at the baroque lettering, flipped the card over in my fingers.

There, scrawled in his Mystery Black chicken-scratch, he had written me a note. I may be the only person on Earth who can decipher his handwriting, but this is what it said:

Bring the dandelion to the tower. Make haste, but do not rush.

We will not require it until after the sun sets, when the chill of darkness settles into the desert.

Yours,

S. C. Scott

PS: Please don't be late. More than you can possibly imagine rides on your good timing.

The Gadget goes off at dawn, if not sooner.

My mouth gaped. It struck me then—the significance of where I stood mushroomed in my mind. I was in White Sands National Monument, somewhere near the Trinity Test Site. Only it wasn't now any more—it was then. The big moment. When the world was forever changed. July 15th, 1945, the eve of thermonuclear madness. The detonation had originally been scheduled for 4:00 a.m. on the 16th, though from my history books I knew it had actually been delayed until about 5:20 in the morning by thunderstorms rolling through the desert.

Still, the explosion had come before dawn. The first rise of a false, evil sun.

And if I couldn't find my way out of this fix, I'd be incinerated with it.

I cursed Sarin Chandrasankar Scott, his expatriate upper-crust English mother, his monsoon of a father—an unordained preacher of some mystical flavor of Catholicism who'd been born and raised in the slums of Mumbai—or Bombay, as it had been known at the time.

Mr. Scott himself had been born on a jetliner caught in the throes of a thunderstorm over Sri Lanka, and I wasn't quite convinced his feet had ever touched down and attached themselves firmly to Mother Earth. Whatever the nature of his soul, it had latched itself instead to those uncertain dimensions, meandering through the world like a threadbare white curtain, that manifest themselves in the occult and the strange. He certainly had done nothing to prove me to the contrary.

For I now understood what he asked of me.

I had to place the dandelion I'd plucked—the twin of the one he had taken with him—under the tower holding the world's first atomic bomb, its deadly payload of plutonium loaded, the fuse ready to be lit.

And I had not the slightest inkling as to why.

* * *

I KEPT PLODDING ONWARD, EVER DEEPER into the sands. The fine-powdered gypsum shifted under my feet, seemed to flee my each and every footfall as my boots struggled to find purchase. It was hard going, and I am a man as fit and limber now as in any of my thirty-six years of life.

I summited one small dune, then another. I spied a hundred and twenty-five foot monster looming just a bit further to the west, and set my sights on summiting it. If I couldn't get my bearings from there, little hope would remain.

The lowest-angled ridge rose up from its south-west side, so I circled around to that. The true angle of the slope could not have been more than five or ten degrees, but it was like trying to walk up a talcum-slicked cliff. For every step I took the sands avalanched back three and the sweltering heat of the sun pounded me back one more for good measure. For long stretches, I made no progress at all, but somehow I slowly, ever slow slowly, made my way toward to its summit. I peeked my head over the top just as the sun settled into the far-off dunes that scalloped the western horizon.

And there it was, clear as a black obelisk standing naked in the sands of Egypt. The steel tower. A hundred-foot trelliswork of crisscrossing steel beams with a tin-roofed lookout tower atop it. Only there were no windows, no doors.

It was the ignition tower. The Gadget was already sealed within, the fuse primed. Man had but to speak the word and the wrath of God would be unleashed upon the pristine white sands.

The Trinity Test Site. A site of sublime mystery, of soon-to-be unfathomable destruction.

The sun winked away behind the horizon, blood crimson creeping into the sky, and I sat down and waited for darkness to take hold of the Jornada del Muerto.

* * *

ALL I HAD TO DO WAS HOLD MY BEARING and I'd come upon the tower. I took Mr. Scott at his word, and knew he'd be there, if only I didn't lose myself in the darkness.

Easier said than done when you're tumbling down an immense dune of gypsum, nothing but a few stars pinpricking the night sky here and there. Clouds were moving in ahead of the storm front, growing denser, and soon there would be nothing to navigate by at all.

I stumbled and slid, I pushed my feet in futility against the sand, moving further along the bearing—I could only hope—where I'd spied the tower. Five hundred yards, one thousand yards, or perhaps a mile or two. I had no real sense of distance or time, not idea of how far I'm come, of how far I'd fallen back.

Finally I gave up and shouted, in the loudest whisper I could muster if that makes any sense, and called out to Mr. Scott. The observation bunkers were some ten kilometers away, I knew, there was no way they could possibly hear me or see me, but still I didn't want to needlessly call attention to myself.

I shouted out again, a little louder, and this time was finally rewarded for my sufferings.

"Morrow! Over here!"

I headed towards the voice, heard more whispering as I drew near. I heard a clink and saw a spark in the darkness, and then the dull orange-yellow flame Mr. Scott's stainless steel lighter licking at the darkness.

"Watch your head," he said, gesturing to a stout iron I-beam angling up into the darkness. He sat back down, cross-legged in a small circle, Mrs. Katani, still in her black-piped white pantsuit and low-cut white leather shoes here in the desert

There was another man I didn't recognize sitting across from them.

He had wide-set pebble eyes behind perfectly round black spectacles. His black hair was close-cropped and slicked back, his nose a bit too long, his nostrils gaping a bit too wide. His lips seemed too fleshy to come properly together, forcing his mouth into a subtle but perpetual frown. He wore a black suit and black tie with a white button-down shirt. He looked very uncomfortable there in his dress shoes and his black wool slacks, sitting Indian-style on the fine white sand.

I had no idea who he was and he hadn't said a thing, but already I didn't like the looks of him. He struck me as a changeling, a doppelganger, a parroter of words.

Mr. Scott gestured to the man with an open palm. "Morrow, this is Klaus Fuchs."

The man offered his hand, weak-looking with spatulate fingers, and I took it reluctantly in my own.

"Gruss gott," he said. *God greet you.*

"Wenn ich ihn sehe," I replied, in my well-rusted German. *If I see him.*

Fuchs drew back and scowled.

I thrust my fists deep into my pockets in return.

Mr. Scott gestured for me to sit. "You have the dandelion, yes?"

I produced it from deep in my pocket, heavily wilted, the flower head sealed up tight with just the back of the dark green petals showing. "Not much to look at, I'm afraid," I said, and handed it over to Mr. Scott.

"No, it's good," he said. "Perfect, even. Just as I hoped. Everything sealed within. Come now, seat yourself."

And with that I sat down cross-legged beside him, as far from Fuchs as I could manage while still joining the conversation, and listened to Mr. Scott long into the shortest night ever there was on this Earth.

* * *

THUNDER RUMBLED IN THE DISTANCE, rattled the loose bolts in the tower capping the darkness above us, but Mr. Scott went on, holding court in absolute darkness punctuated by distant heartbeats of lightning. I could smell the approaching downpour on the desiccated gypsum air.

"There was no choice," he finally said, working his way around to the heart of the matter. "We had to recruit Klaus. Shizuko-sensei had to tell him her story. Hans Bethe said it himself—Klaus Fuchs was 'the only physicist I know who truly changed history.' And so it is. Isn't that right, Klaus?"

"So long as only one nation holds zee secret atomic, all nations in peril lie. 'Man is zee cruelest animal,' yes? Nietzsche always says eet best: 'be careful when you fight zee monsters, lest you become one.' And vith zees bomb, zee Monster now is you, America. Zee Soviets need to know. In zees, I have no shame."

"That may be so," Mr. Scott said, with a great clap of his hands, "and what is done cannot be undone. But by way of restitution, he shall help us one last time, in the matter that now confronts us."

Mr. Scott flicked on his lighter once more and reached into his inside suit-coat pocket, pulled out his tin of snuff. Twisted off the lid, dipped the now-empty tin in the gypsum sand. Let the incredibly fine pure-white particles pour in, fill up the emptiness within.

He put the lid back on and handed it to Fuchs. "For the fat man," Mr. Scott said. "A pinch will do. We need nothing else but your silence."

Fuchs glowered at Mr. Scott from behind his glasses with those periscoped eyes, but at length he gave a small curt nod. "I vill do eet," he said, and took the tin in his fist. "You have my vord."

And with that Fuchs marched off petulantly into the desert.

He still had hours to reach the bunker. I could not imagine that Fuchs was a popular man. I was certain that nobody had noticed him missing in the excitement of the defining moment that loomed before them. The moment that would 'make them become Death, the destroyer of worlds,' in the justly famous words of Oppenheimer.

When Fuchs was gone I asked the question that needed to be asked. "What makes you so sure he'll cooperate?"

"He's a traitor and a spy. A man with a worm-eaten will. He'll bring down the great Oppenheimer, cast a cloud even over the brilliant and charismatic Feynman. If I were to expose Fuchs now, he would be executed at daybreak. If not sooner. People disappear in the desert all the time."

"Yes, I'm sure. But who's this 'fat man,' and why's he need the sand?"

Mr. Scott laughed gently, but a serious look quickly came over him once more as he realized the gravity of the moment. "Why nobody, Morrow, nobody t'all. The Fat Man is not a person. It is the bomb to be detonated over Nagasaki, and Klaus Fuchs will conceal a pinch of the Trinity sands within it for us. That way, when it detonates, it will draw our leylines taut from here to the skies of Japan. To the light that falls upon a certain gazebo in a Japanese garden in Nagasaki, at the very instant before it was vaporized."

Mrs. Katani started weeping silently, and Mr. Scott consoled her. After she had stopped, after a long respectful silence, I pursued the matter that troubled me so deeply.

"Why on Earth would you do that? Why not have him defuse it, have him sabotage it in some inconspicuous way?"

"He'd surely be discovered, for one. And second, you can't change history, not really, not like that. There are limits to this synchronicity, these leylines we've entangled ourselves with. There are causes and effects beyond our reach— information, once destroyed, is lost forever. We can't undo what's been done; the universe simply doesn't work that way."

His lips assumed a troubled frown, he clenched his jaw hard and long. "We can't bring back the dead from the beyond. They are gone. Forever."

The ominous rumbling in the distance was nearly upon us. The peals of thunder were becoming sharp and distinct. Lightning veined the black mushrooming contours of the thunderheads in the night.

It was time.

Shizuko-sensei lifted her clamshell purse from her lap, snapped open the gilded clasp. Her fingers reverently slipped into the white leather folds, emerged holding a squat, square-profiled incense candle and a small glass vial.

Mr. Scott lit the wick and the flame flickered to life. It smelled of vanilla and persimmon and other exotic spices far beyond my conception.

I could see better now the vial. It was of transparent glass and stopped with a bamboo cork. Sealed within was a clear liquid.

Shizuko-sensei cleared her throat, spoke up tall and proud. "Rukoko-chan, these tears, I cry for you. I save for this day."

And with that she pulled out the stopper. It came out not with a pop but with a sigh of shallow breath, with a sound like the exhalation of a sleeping infant.

Mr. Scott spun the closed-up dandelion in his fingers, caressed the broken end of its stem with the palm of his other hand, and dropped it into the water.

It was the cleanest, purest, most sacred water I have ever set my eyes upon. The dandelion, slowly but surely, drew open its florets like a blossoming sun.

And with that, in the blink of an eye, we sat cross-legged on the cool gray slate tiles lining the floor of a wrought-iron gazebo. In the distance, a pagoda crowned a dense stand of conifers, and above that, from a gap in the clouds, a pinprick of blinding light pierced the sky. Beyond, the silhouette of a bomber banked away from Nagasaki. It was August 9th, 1945, just after eleven o'clock in the morning.

And here, within the wrought-iron gazebo, a bundle of white blankets lay on a low dark-stained teakwood bench.

From within, hushed by the pure white linen, issued the unmistakable coos of an infant.

* * *

IT WAS NOT UNTIL I NOTICED THE FLOCK of swifts, back-lit motionless in the sky, that I realized the world was frozen. Trapped in an instant.

I turned to look behind me. A black-haired man, short but standing erect and proud as the pagoda in the distance, stood at the railing, clutching the black iron in his fists. He stood absolutely without movement, a living statue of himself. He looked out over the arboretum, towards the silhouette of the bomber fleeing to the horizon.

Time had stopped all around us. Except for the baby. Except for ourselves. I wanted to ask Mr. Scott why, but I dared not disturb the moment. It was all that we had, and it belonged to Mrs. Katani.

Sometimes you just have to trust him, Mr. Scott. Serendipity was on his side, and he always found a way to work things out, found a way to bring order to chaos.

I held my tongue and looked on as Shizuko-sensei, mouth wide, eyes streaming tears down the deeply furrowed age of her cheeks, rose unsteadily to her feet.

She walked to the baby, to her long-lost sister. Rukoko-chan, her twin, their fates entangled since birth. She hugged the bundle to her chest, wordlessly swayed the infant back and forth, back and forth.

I could watch no more. I closed my eyes to hold back my own tears, my own losses long locked deep inside. But it was not my time, not my hour of revelation. This instant, the hour it took, was hers.

I clenched my eyes tight, bowed my head, and prayed.

* * *

WHEN THE TIME HAD COME, when the moment had drawn to a close, Mr. Scott hugged both of us close and whispered the Lord's Prayer. He is not a religious man, I know this for a fact, but he is a man of reverence with the backbone to stand up and right whatever needs to be righted in this great sad world of ours. But it doesn't always have to be that way. Leylines and fates can be untangled, and faces can smile again.

Mrs. Katani's cheeks were not dry, but she had found her moment, and a dandelion glow lit her flesh from within, bequeathed a solemn hush to her sobs.

Mr. Scott produced the dandelion one last time. Its blossom had gone to seed, the frozen white seed-heads a perfect crystalline sphere of hope.

My breath caught in my throat.

The great man paused one last moment, inhaled deeply, and got ready to blow.

* * *

WHEN I TOOK MY NEXT BREATH I stood once again before the spar-varnished fir planks of the bench in the park, the dandelions folding into themselves as the sun dipped below the horizon.

Mr. Scott helped Shizuko-sensei to her car, ushered her into her seat with a hug and profusion of deep bows. I gave them their distance; I know my place. There are times where the assistant, no matter how helpful, must not intrude.

He walked back with that slow walk of his when he's lost in reflection, heel to heel, a wistful stagger.

I put it to him. "What just happened there? How in the hell did you pull that one off?"

He reached for his snuff tin, only to realize it was gone, that it had vanished with Fuchs into the desert.

"It was the white sand," he said. "Collected by Klaus Fuchs on the eve of the Trinity. *He was there.* Carried it away in the snuff tin, the very same one which eventually came into my possession. And that was the last trace that remained of the actual sand grains that had rested at the foot of the tower. Before the atomic blast turned it all into vast crater, crusted with radioactive glass. That's it—that's all that it was.

"Shizuko-sensei was an infant at the moment of the Nagasaki blast—she had no idea of where her sister was, only that it was a park with a gazebo, location unknown, a place lost to history. The only thing certain was that the gazebo had been vaporized, nothing more than molten heap of slag to mark where it had been—if even that— to memorialize where her sister had lived the last moment of her life. We needed something specific—something concrete. Something entangled with the exact time and location. But no such object existed.

"So instead I used the white sand, and thereby summoned the connection we needed into existence. Mixed the white sand with my snuff, spilled both onto the dandelions. An old Shinto trick, lost to myself and to history alike until Shizuko-sensei came along. She was there— she was entangled with that moment. Her tears. I used the tears to open the dandelion, I used the white sands to bring us back to the Jornada del Muerto—and then I blackmailed Fuchs to put it in the Nagasaki bomb for us, and he came through, the scoundrel. From here to Trinity, from there to Nagasaki, our leylines pulled taut by the pinch of gypsum sand vaporized with the detonation of the Fat Man bomb. It brought us there, gave Shizuko-sensei her moment, and my snuff brought us back. Yes, you heard right Morrow—my white snuff. That too was in my tin, mixed with the sand; that too settled into the dandelion and became entangled with time."

I had more questions for him—there would always be more for the master—but I'd found over the years that I just had to trust in the process, be willing to throw my fate to the vicissitudes of serendipity. And he had done me right so far, and there was always that next conquest or caper awaiting us just beyond the horizon.

Sarin Chandrasankar Scott, the Great Serendipity himself, reached down for the turf. Only then did I notice that the dandelion was still there, gone to seed. The one, the exact same one.

He picked it out of the grass ever so gently, lifted it to his lips, and blew.

A gentle summer breeze moved through my hair, and the dandelion seeds danced off, the fates of so many souls on the wind.

ABOUT THE AUTHOR

WRITER AND WORKING SCIENTIST Ken Hinckley resides in the Seattle area with his wife and children. His fiction appears in professional markets including *Nature*, *Penumbra*, and *Fiction River*, and his research career spans some 80 scientific papers and 150 patents (and counting). He believes he may yet have a good idea or two left in him.

You can find him at kenhinckley.wordpress.com.

ALSO BY
KEN HINCKLEY

Science Fiction and Fantasy

The Totem of Curtained Minds
The Ostracons of Europa
Great Red
Between Grief and Remembrance
First Movement and Other Stories
Bilking Time
Feathers of Frost, Feathers of Flame
The Mistress of Underwater Bats
The Stevedore of Ruined Veils
The Sensei of Dandelions Hushed

Mystery, Crime, and Mainstream

The Blood Red Clay of Old Virginia
The Case of the Waterstained Scarab
Dead All These Years
The Miles
The Steward of Perfect Obscurity
Mappa Mundi

ELECTRONIC COPY

For a free copy of this book in any electronic form for any device, please go to:

www.smashwords.com/books/view/351540

And then when you check out, enter the code:

AR24V

This will allow you to download your free electronic copy of this story in any format you pick.